The Principles of Life
on Black Friday

THE GERMAN LIST

WORKS OF ALEXANDER KLUGE AVAILABLE FROM SEAGULL BOOKS

Russia Container
Translated by Alexander Booth

Kong's Finest Hour
A Chronicle of Connections
Translated by Cyrus Shahan, Kai-Uwe Werbeck, Susanne Gomoloch, Emma Woelk, Martin Brady, Helen Hughes and Robert Blankenship

Anyone Who Utters a Consoling Word Is a Traitor
Translated by Alta L. Price

World-Changing Rage
News of the Antipodeans
With GEORG BASELITZ
Translated by Katy Derbyshire

The Labyrinth of Tender Force
166 Love Stories
Translated by Wieland Hoban

Drilling through Hard Boards
133 Political Stories
Translated by Wieland Hoban

Dispatches from Moments of Calm
89 Stories, 64 Pictures
With GERHARD RICHTER
Translated by Nathaniel McBride

December
39 Stories, 39 Pictures
With GERHARD RICHTER
Translated by Martin Chalmers

30 April 1945
The Day Hitler Shot Himself and Germany's Integration with the West Began
Translated by Wieland Hoban

Air Raid
On Halberstadt on 8 April 1945
Translated by Martin Chalmers

The Principles of Life on Black Friday

CHRONICLE OF EMOTIONS

NOTEBOOK 1

ALEXANDER KLUGE

TRANSLATED BY
MARTIN CHALMERS and RICHARD LANGSTON

LONDON NEW YORK CALCUTTA

This publication was supported by a grant from
the Goethe-Institut India

Seagull Books, 2023

First published in German as Alexander Kluge,
Der Eigentümer und seine Zeit in Chronik der Gefühle, Band I

First published in English translation by Seagull Books, 2023

ISBN 978 1 8030 9 224 9

British Library Cataloguing-in-Publication Data
A catalogue record for this book is available from the British Library

Typeset at Seagull Books, Calcutta, India
Printed and bound by Hyam Enterprises, Calcutta, India

CONTENTS

A Foreword with Three Images

Notebook 1 is the first of nine in a series entitled CHRONICLE OF EMOTIONS. This first instalment concerns itself with TIME: 'the body of water in which all life transpires'.

The stories contained in this notebook begin with the description of a fragment, 0.0001 per cent of a person's lifetime, which transpires in a matter of seconds. It concludes with stories about the unexpected stock market crash of 1929, a once-in-a-hundred-year event that Europeans call *Black Friday*.[1]

These stories narrate their tales from the perspective of emotions (*sentiments*). This is why they belong to a 'chronicle of emotions'. Emotions are the true inhabitants of human lives. They reside in people just as people live in houses. We are, in brief, 'dwellings made of time'. From within these houses, emotions gaze out onto history, objective events and the outside world that rages around them.

Inside and out, the world has always been obscure. In our age, we've reached, however, a new kind of obscurity. We've encountered the virus. We saw the strange costumes worn at the Capitol riot on 6 January 2021. In 2022, we see before us

---

1 The Wall Street Crash of 1929 took place on Thursday, 24 October of that year and was often referred to in the United States as 'Black Thursday'. The effects of that unprecedented sell-off on Wall Street reached Europe one day later and was known there as 'Black Friday'. Without Black Friday there would be no Hitler. While Black Thursday is no longer as common as the 'Great Crash' or the 'Great Depression' once were, Black Friday evokes very different associations in Europe today than it once did: on the one hand, it is an annual call to consumerism and, on the other, it is a lingering European perspective on world-changing historical events. [Trans.]

inflation and war. This is 'life in our times'. We look at the world with suspense: this is worthy of a chronicle.

What can I trust? How can I protect myself? What should I be afraid of? What holds voluntary action together? These are fundamental questions not altered by the passing of time alone and that constitute a true chronicle.

What humans need in their lives is ORIENTATION. Just like ships that navigate the high seas. This is the function of all the stories in my CHRONICLE OF EMOTIONS. Because a book is like a mirror, readers will invariably compare the stories in the following pages. Sometimes readers will be repelled and at other times they will be drawn in.

We humans have two kinds of property: our life spans and our obstinacy. This is what these stories are about.

A.K.

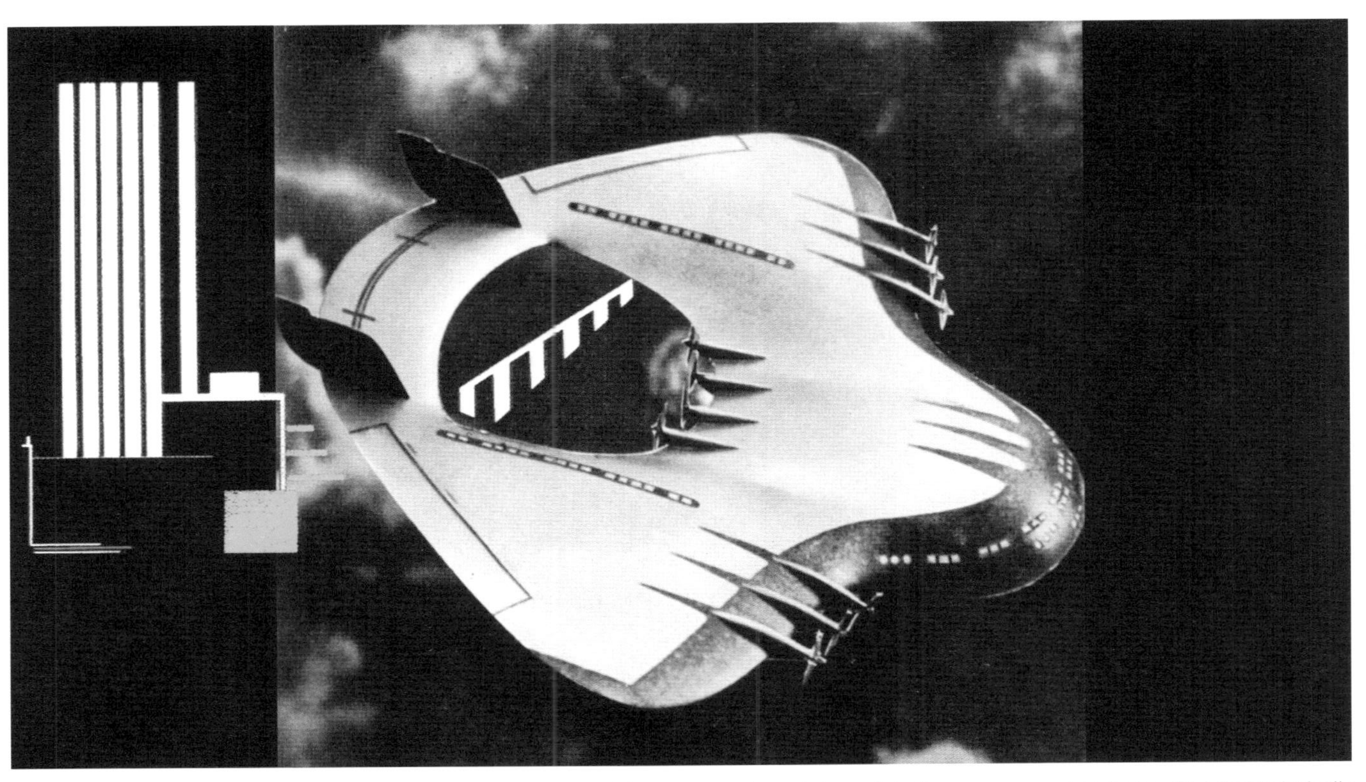

FIGURE 1. 'Great expectations one hundred years ago.' The year of the great stock market crash is the same year when hopes for a technologically advanced modernity thrived.

FIGURE 2. Horror that history repeats itself today so clumsily. An animal from Walter Benjamin's favourite book—Bertuch's *Bilderbuch für Kinder* from 1807—observes the destruction in Ukraine in the illustration above.

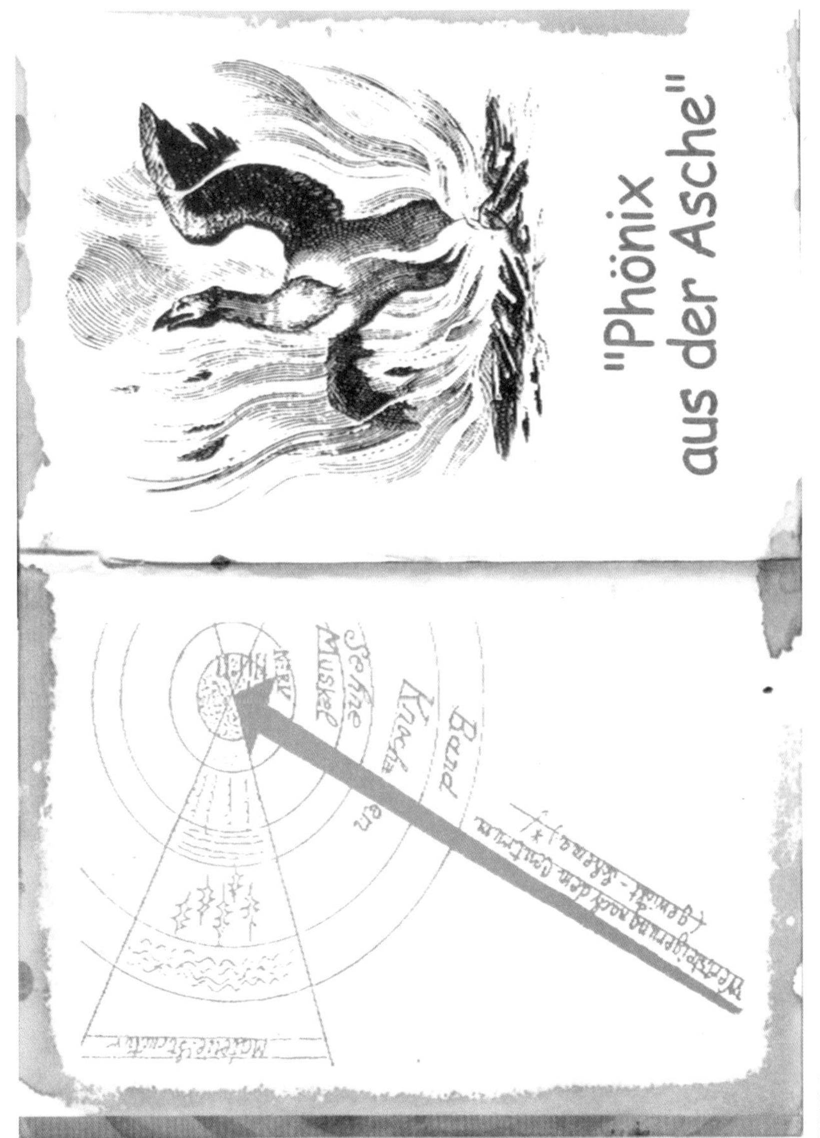

FIGURE 3

0.0001 per cent of a Lifetime

With his shoulders bent, the innkeeper of Brusquetta d'Agneau is hunched over his newspaper and his café au lait. His wife draws his attention to the altercation between three dogs in the house entrance opposite them. Now the dogs have disappeared. The innkeeper is still looking (in the lethargy of the morning) at the door, through which they disappeared into the house (squabbling to the last). With an indifferent curious expression in his eyes, he turns his head to the side for a total of 31 seconds. He now shifts his field of vision to the newspaper. A long forenoon's journey until the arrival of the lunchtime guests. The innkeeper has used up less than 0.0001 per cent of his lifetime for his sideways glance at the dogs.

An Afternoon on the Ligurian Coast

An afternoon in a city on the coast of Liguria. To reach the office of notary R., one has to climb up a marble staircase. The notary spends the afternoon in accordance with the habits of all his days (except on holidays) by recording brief notarial declarations and occasionally telling stories that brighten up his mood; meanwhile, documents are presented, read aloud and returned. The subsequent course of minutes is enriched with stories. He livens up while telling a story, his pulse, which slows down when reading business documents aloud, begins to speed up. This is how his employees outside have time to assemble the documents. With the passing of the years, the flow of his narrative interruptions became so smooth that by the end of such a work session all the documents requiring a signature were processed. Information about expenses, notary fees and land transfer duties along with his brief narrative observations lasted exactly long enough to complete the final page of the documents where the signatures belonged. Since his return from the University of Bologna, this is how he spends his days (except on holidays), as his father, grandfather and their forerunners did before him. On the wall, above the head of the Genoese notary, there's a picture of his ancestor from 1804 ('Il mio antinato'). His children and grandchildren were outside in the corridor. They all became notaries who helped facilitate the acquisition of land in much the same way a country doctor watches over births. Like the trickling sand in an hourglass, six generations measure the time of the city. Uncoupled from the majority of developments in this world, this time drifts through the centuries as if it were asleep.

A Case of Time Pressure

On Kaiserstrasse in Frankfurt am Main, schools for continuing education, places of prostitution, fast food joints and exotic restaurants stand next to one another. The attention of the passer-by hurrying towards the train station is drawn less by the branch offices of airlines, for example, sandwiched in between these establishments because they only speak to specialized interests. In 1982, one of the big banks in the city located its West African division opposite the hotel Frankfurter Hof. After work, the head of this division, Ingmar B., made his way to the station by foot. There were no suitable parking places in the vicinity of his office. It was easier to get to his home near Kronberg by train.

For a time, Frankfurt's police didn't know how to deal with the Marseilles-based group of pimps who controlled the prostitutes around Frankfurt's central station. The gang recruited young women from the villages in former French Guinea and then had specialists from Marseilles instruct them in a certain kind of course for two years in quarters located in the side streets off of Kaiserstrasse. Compared with the standards of their homeland, they earned a fortune. These transactions are only possible with the consent of the village elders; the procedures for these agreements, the sums of money and guarantees are all standardized. They assume that the women are returned to West Africa unharmed. It's about a kind of *ius primae noctis* for white men in the metropolis organized by white men who, after the end of colonial rule, built up a 'specific relationship to violence': a form of fixed-term slavery that handles its objects with care. If one of the gang members were accustomed to reflection or discussion, then the familial background, the strong ROOTEDNESS IN MUTUAL CONSENT underlying loyalties within the gang and the laws of trustworthiness in the trafficking of human beings from West Africa would swiftly come to light. Conversely, the mighty flows of finance directed from desks in a metropolis like Frankfurt, among others, structure the life zones of southern France or West Africa in a much more ruthless way. Their behaviour is marked by indifference. Like a weather phenomenon, they take hold of territories and tribes without ever negotiating with village elders, settling on guarantees or assuming the obligation of repatriating human beings in the event they are sucked up and then spat out again by the flow of money.

Department head Ingmar B. fell for one of the African prostitutes, whom the gang had established in Moselstrasse, with a deadly outcome. It was not a matter, as he assumed, of sexual intercourse in return for money. He got to know the young girl named Gilla—she also went by the name Françoise (she probably had a completely different name at home; at times B. took her for a chieftain's daughter, an 'enchanted princess' whose ancestors, he thought, reached back to eighteenth-century Africa)—at a pub called Reichsstuben. He spoke to her and at first supposed his interest to be business-like. Since he was also responsible for West Africa, it was interesting to make the acquaintance of a resident of this region and to enchant her for a magical late afternoon for a dirt-cheap fee (judging by his means). Since his imagination, without him noticing in time, was powerfully stimulated, he was in top form; he believed that something of his own pleasure was being passed on to his foreign partner. She spoke French.

In the weeks that followed—it was November and Advent was beginning—Ingmar developed an 'inescapable dependence' on the foreign woman. He would leave his office at about one in the afternoon already and look for her in town. He spent one night with her in a bar, causing his family in Kronberg to contact police headquarters and request a search in the dead of night. At 5 a.m., the special investigation team at the train station found him under the influence of champagne at a bar called Lobos. He succeeded in hushing up the incident. His wife forgave him, although she hardly had a clue as to what it was about.

In January, the time was approaching when the young woman was due to be taken back to her village in West Africa, as was originally agreed. Her handlers tried carefully to push Ingmar away. They offered him substitutes. They made it difficult for him to find his beloved. When he did track her down (he was helped by acquaintances from the train station's special investigation team), he implored her (Gilla's statements of consent were valid only to the extent that she understood his plans) to start a new life with him. He often thought of changing jobs, of giving everything up.

On the day before Christmas Eve, he runs into the legal adviser from the Marseilles gang who takes him to task: he must give up the search for the young woman immediately. The woman's repatriation—that she be returned unharmed and on time—was a law that must not be violated, not in this particular case and certainly not on account of HOW LIFE IS IMAGINED IN THE METROPOLE. It was up to Ingmar, whether he wanted to woo his beauty in her homeland and in accordance with its rules. As Ingmar knew, that was futile. The village elders accepted neither whites nor strangers.

He talked all the more insistently to his beloved in the hours they spent together. She was under pressure from her handlers. At the office where he was regularly missing, an internal audit was ordered. The decision as to what kind of life he should lead, what life at all and under what external circumstances, had to be made very quickly. Christmas was the day after tomorrow and it seemed unimaginable to him to spend so many solitary days in Kronberg imprisoned with his family, to 'live a lie', so to speak, so far from life itself. He had 48 hours left until the children were given their Christmas presents, a very short time in which to put his life in order. Agitated by the time pressure, he shot at one of the Marseilles pimps who tried in the bar to get Françoise to break off her sojourn with Ingmar. He pushed the young woman towards the exit when Ingmar fired seven times. All that was left of the criminal, who had no residence permit, was a sticky mess where his head and chest once were. Françoise disappeared (no one in Frankfurt ever saw her again; it may be assumed that she was flown out). Ingmar had borrowed the revolver from a detective who owed him a favour. He shot himself in the men's toilet in the bar, while the course of tragic events was still being reconstructed by the police officers on call. The bar's liquor licence was revoked.

As he was filling out the death certificate, Dr Fritzsche of forensic remarked that the head of the bank's West African division possessed sufficient competence to transform that area of the globe into a flourishing region, to organize, so to speak, a leap out of the African Middle Ages and into modem times. How odd, he said, that an influence from a place he ruled over to a certain extent should kill him. Could this romance have had a happy ending without the time pressure before Christmas Eve? he asked himself. All those on duty at the crime scene were waiting for two experts from homicide and had time to talk. It's unlikely that it would have worked out, said Detective Inspector Schmücker. Why do all love affairs end tragically? Not all, replied Schmücker. But always those under time pressure.

A Conversation between Detective Inspector Schmücker and Forensic Expert Dr Fritzsche

'A trace of life.'

'It's from long ago.'

'Limits of a causal perspective.'

'What is a love trap?'

They stood around as they had an unexpected amount of time on their hands. They had earned this island of time quite legitimately on account of erroneous planning. As long as the unhappy perpetrator was alive, it had been correct to assume that here they were dealing with a 'big case with sensational headlines in the tabloid press'. With the suicide of the perpetrator, however, the picture had changed.

The two friends sat down at one of the little tables. The kitchen staff, already unemployed due to the closure of the bar, served them drinks. This team, too, was not yet ready to admit its loss of function.

SCHMÜCKER. Now was the fact that he fired the gun and then turned it on himself a short circuit? He wouldn't have got more than a two-year suspended sentence, and a smart lawyer might even have turned it into a case of self-defence or putative self-defence. Or would he, had he more time at his disposal, always return to this despair until the day he died?

DR FRITZSCHE. I've never known it like that because *after* Christmas, in the course of January, everything dies down and returns to normal. It's forgotten.

SCHMÜCKER. What is an *amour fou* worth if it's forgotten?

DR FRITZSCHE. It probably doesn't end, instead it slumps downward. I can't exclude the possibility that it's bad for your health.

SCHMÜCKER. Cancer?

DR FRITZSCHE. As far as we know, the link isn't as direct as that. Can also be a sore throat, or you don't notice anything external at all.

SCHMÜCKER. But it's stored up, even while it's out of one's mind?

DR FRITZSCHE. I assume so.

SCHMÜCKER. After the necessary number of upheavals of the soul, the individual trace of life returns to the spot where it was once kindled. But the life of a mortal human being is too short for him to experience this return himself.

DR FRITZSCHE. That's exactly the way I see it. I once had a case where there was no sign of life any more. And one day the woman drives into a tree. It was irrational.

SCHMÜCKER. Strange. Why did he only have eyes for the Black woman? Presumably not because it was his area of professional responsibility.

DR FRITZSCHE. It's like a package, already prepared. It bangs shut on him.

SCHMÜCKER. Could it have anything to do with the fact that this was a 'fake prostitute'? She appears in our strange world as if it were none of her business, soulless devotion, so to speak. The idle soul of the victim stumbles into this vacuum or pit, you might say.

DR FRITZSCHE. That's a pretty accurate description of the course of events. The missing woman leads a double life. We're familiar with that from sylphs, mermaids, etc.

SCHMÜCKER. Is there any point in conducting a search for the missing woman?

DR FRITZSCHE. What would we do with her if we found her?

SCHMÜCKER. I would certainly like to question her.

DR FRITZSCHE. But you couldn't put it on file.

SCHMÜCKER. No.

DR FRITZSCHE. There's nothing she can be prosecuted for.

SCHMÜCKER. Perhaps for entering the country illegally?

DR FRITZSCHE. So what?

SCHMÜCKER. 'Illegal entry with fatal consequences for a respected citizen of the Federal Republic—'

DR FRITZSCHE. Not a punishable offence.

SCHMÜCKER. Would witchcraft be punishable if it existed?

DR FRITZSCHE. Sure.

SCHMÜCKER. But it doesn't exist.

DR FRITZSCHE. Exactly!

The two detectives from homicide now arrived; they had been called in from the get-go because of the importance of the case. The coffee cups and saucers piled up on the little table where the forensic doctor and the detective inspector were waiting. They kept themselves 'alert' with caffeine throughout the afternoon, maintaining a distance from hazy dreams as long as they were on duty: they were nevertheless inspired to dream. Their colleagues from homicide had all the details of the incident, which was forensically complicated but without any consequence in terms of criminal law, presented to them yet again simply because they had come a long way and were not prepared to consider their activity futile. Now the dead banker could be taken away. The family had to be informed.

A Commentary on Anna Karenina

There is an elementary force that cannot be deciphered from the impressions of confused reason and especially not from those of a confused heart. This is why the face of the child who just visited Anna Karenina was distended.

She met her betrayed, stubborn husband, who kicked her out of the house. A disaster. But the governess watched the child, who cried for several hours without eating. She was concerned. At the same time, she distrusted her powers of observation and thought her vision was too sharp. She didn't immediately call the family doctor.

But the boy's features grew spongy. The left side of the head was excessively distended, as is the case with severe inflammation. It was possible that it had to do with an infected cut on his forehead, a wound he touched with his soiled fingers that had just wiped away his tears.

The catastrophic change in the child's face was soon obvious to the governess. She ran to the master of the house and alerted the servants. The doctor summoned did not want to decide on a diagnosis. The strange clinical picture was unclear to him. The tears were still streaming down the sides of the disfigured 'chubby face', running along the immeasurable swelling; the frightfulness of the child's apparition shocked his father. He sent for Anna Karenina. His calculating, 'cold-hearted' spirit didn't want to be accused of having kicked his wife out of the house and then immediately afterwards their child dies. The messenger reached the young woman, who hurried to install herself in the boy's room as if she wanted to stay there forever. Even though the doctor couldn't give a diagnosis, the monstrous cheek, which had just looked like the result of an outrageous smack on the face, receded after a few days. Anna Karenina did not leave the house again. The old man left things in this unspoken, improvised state, in which nothing was resolved and between the spouses there was no peace. He makes a series of eloquent attempts to reconnect with Anna Karenina. Anna Karenina feared heavenly punishment, injury to her son. In her confused state, the life of her child seemed like something she had spawned, something more elemental than a love story. She remembered reading a very similar story in a novel that ended fatally.[2] But the child could do magic. Just as it would look in death, his closed eyes exhibited an expression of peace.

Blood like Bubbling Water

> 'It had to bubble up like a spring. As ideas bubble, when one is in good company. For that, said the doctor, I would have to puncture your carotid artery; a broad longitudinal section—then you'll see it bubble. The patient laughed.'
>
> Alexander Pushkin

He had seen his blood in the test tube. It was like honey, glutinous. That's a mass of cholesterol, said the internist. It flows

2 It was a French novel. It was not kept in the house. For that reason, she only had a memory of it. She no longer sought violent solutions. For this reason, she didn't have to die on the tracks of a train station; she didn't even find out what her fate would have been. Her blood flowed through her veins. It was not a prison where she lived.

sluggishly like syrup through your veins. It no longer penetrates the capillaries at all, but rather wets them where they branch off.

The doctor was in the habit of showing his patients samples of their innards. He wanted to increase their dependence on his authority. Like addicts, they returned to his office. They obeyed his instructions. They were his sinecures.

This manager, for example, had no self-confidence, as long as he suspected, that the sluggish substance, which flowed in him like blood, still had the honey-like consistency he had seen in the test tube. He came to the doctor's office once a week. He sought to accelerate his 'recuperation' by bribing the doctor with presents. He could only imagine 'quick decisions', as they were demanded of him as a manager, if his blood flowed pink like raspberry juice. He would not have even tolerated the bulges of thin fluid that appear at the edges where it stops flowing and forms drops. He wanted to have, he said, *strictly flat blood.*[3] That doesn't exist in nature, and so the doctor didn't show him any of the samples of his meanwhile regenerated blood, liquefied by several decimal points. It's never reminiscent of raspberry juice, not even in pathological cases. But always of honey (which of course has various consistencies) or 'speedy' red syrup.

Emotion Consists of What Remains Unused

Gerda held a lobster tail in her fist and gnawed on it. The sun beat down on the ocean. Gerda wants to let Katrin, who is crouching on a mound of sand in front of the canopied beach chair, bite off a piece. Katrin is, however, surprised that she is being noticed at all and assumes that she is to get all of the fairly

3 The term 'flat' comes from advertising. It refers to a 'flat stomach'. When the curvature, even in the case of very runny fluids, forms drops, it is a consequence of physics.

expensive lobster tail. She says: No, I'll keep it for little Karl. Little Karl is her son, who would be pleased with the tail. Not the whole tail, says Gerda; she clears up her friend's mistake: she just wants to let her have a bite, she wants to give her a little piece. Oh, I see, replies Katrin. She's embarrassed that she appears so greedy. Now the lobster tail has accidentally fallen into the sand and the women have to walk down to the ocean to clean it.

While walking together, the two clear up the situation from the last few minutes by rearranging some of their memories. A pleasurable harmony arises: They could explore the split-second events, which the misunderstanding triggered, and now even talk them over without embarrassment, but this they don't do because it's already become unnecessary on account of how they sense that they possess something of interest. It's worth studying while their feet splash around in the shallow water. This thing worth studying is preserved precisely because it is not discussed any further. Such an intermediate stage between clarification and non-clarification is an emotion that strikes a balance.

Taking the whole snack for oneself (the suddenness of ownership had the effect that Gerda wanted to save it up, thereby prolonging it for herself so that her little son, too, will be as surprised by the lobster tail as she has been) is a STATE OF SUSPENSE shot through in a flash by whole decades of scrimping. Such a flash is worth 10,000 lobster tails. But something like that happens only on the condition that she has never before been offered such a fishy piece of meat. To swallow it brings the emotion to an end, just as explicit clarification would bring the happy moment to an end, in which the two women walk back up from the water to the beach chair. Who should eat the tail now? Neither of the two much wants to. Gerda wraps up the cleaned leftovers. It has no further use.

Shortly after the start of the discussion, which held him back because the late show was delayed as a result, projectionist Sigrist got the following impression: members of the audience who asked to speak did not do so in order to communicate something, but rather to prove themselves in front of the famous guest. The latter, in turn, spoke or replied for the sake of the test, which he wanted to pass in front of the audience. To projectionist Sigrist, that seemed as superfluous as 'waiting for the sun to rise'. He knew a teacher who voluntarily stood up at three in the morning 'to experience the sunrise'. The point was to confront pupils, who associated a vague idea with 'sunrise' in the line of a poem, with solid information. Up to that point, nothing in the world could have persuaded them to rise at 3 a.m. and investigate light conditions before sunrise. They were not curious. So the teacher did it on their behalf. But it was not possible for him to share the sunrise he had seen with his pupils. By about 8 a.m., it had disappeared. There remained only the words of his report. They meant nothing to the sleepy, uninterested pupils. They made an effort in light of the trouble their teacher had gone to and wanted to prove themselves to him by cracking their eyes open wide. Just as he had proved himself by being an exemplary early riser.

Sigrist, on the other hand, knew what a sunrise looked like thanks to an Australian film set in South Africa. There the sun rose at about 4.30 a.m., emerged out of the Asiatic regions of the ocean like a colossus, from India above rocky peaks on the coast. Across from the sun, two men, unjustly condemned to death, sat on cafe chairs with their backs to the West.[4] The squad drawn up in the East shot them along with their chairs.

The film had scratches. It had been sent to the cinema by mistake. The projectionist would have had the time and known

4 The cafe chairs had been borrowed by the firing squad.

how to restore the copy. He would have been prepared to work on the scratches, which were on the shiny side, and thus make out of a damaged copy a first-class scratch-free sunrise at 4.30 a.m. But he didn't want to do it just so that an untalented projectionist in another location could produce scratches once again (possibly in different places). He would only have done it if he alone had been allowed to project the impeccable sunrise on the screen. That, however, would have offended the pecking order since the copy first had to be shown in a category A cinema before it could be released for this house, which was in category B.[5]

The projectionist bemoaned the length of the discussion, which blocked the cinema auditorium. It was not at all about concrete things like a 'sunrise' or 'scratches'. He could only wait by doing nothing. The discussion was going on at his expense since he would now get to bed about three-quarters of an hour later. He would have regarded this hassle as justified only for the projection of an absolutely scratch-free copy of any film you like. Sigrist was considered fussy as far as the quality of films went. The film surface should show no splices or damage to the image surface. Since practically no such impeccable copies existed, he loathed the content of movies and the destructive habit of leading discussions in the cinema for the sake of proving oneself and punishing others. Because he knew that a time machine like cinema cannot make up for lost time by way of discussion (as a locomotive engineer does on account of a delay), he avenged the built-up annoyance he felt at the various misuses of the movie theatre by omitting Acts 4 and 5 from the crime film scheduled for the late show. There was indeed a jump in the plot, which as far as Sigrist was concerned clearly improved the film.

5 Since the 1930s, cinemas in Germany have been divided into categories. A film must, first of all, be shown in the higher category before a distributor is allowed to rent it out to the lower category.

He would have liked to have had the job of generally improving films this way, but he realized that to do so he would have to make cuts in the films. It wasn't always a matter of leaving out whole acts.[6] But then there would be splices that, even if he carefully painted over the soundtrack with Indian ink, produced ugly blemishes. He was not prepared to accept faults in the copy for the sake of more beautiful content. Ultimately, he thought, the content was arbitrary, the quality of the copy, however, is the road along which all content, interchangeable or not, moved. He was neither prepared to concede on this radical question nor was he prepared to waste his nights on something relative (= half good).

After the end of the screening, he packed his bag after he had wound back the copy of the late film and prepared it to be shipped. He was very surprised that copies of films were not used as fodder.

Causality Outstripped

Imagine, said Mrs Hilde Böhlecke, that the snow, which comes down from Prins Christianssund in the far north, is poisoned. But I don't die right away, rather I perish in eight weeks' time because the poison acts slowly. Nevertheless, I am not afraid because my apartment is nice and warm. She wanted to send a postcard, dressed herself and was run over by a car on the corner of Tengstrasse and Adelheidstrasse. Hence the prospect of death in a Third World War made no difference to her.

But some of her cells lived for another few days and conferred with one another as to what the event could very well mean. We don't agree, they said, that masses of snow moving in from

---

6 As a rule, a feature film consists of 10 rolls, which are combined into two rolls of 5 acts each.

Greenland could be poisonous. In our opinion, they say, Mrs Böhlecke had a right to her own death. She does not have to put up, therefore, with a protracted death threatened by snowfall that is deceptively similar to the Christ child, even if a completely different death has meanwhile occurred and the question is apparently outdated.

As long as they still have a spark of life in them, individual human cells are legal scholars in disguise. They thirst for water and then for a piece of justice on earth.

On the question of causality outstripped: In 1936 a wealthy man was sailing to America on a steamer. He had a box of cigars. They were stolen from him by a poorer man called Eike. After that, the ship was damaged by an iceberg and sank. Once he had been saved, Mr Eike, the smart thief, said in his defence: The box of cigars would have gone down anyway. It makes no difference—considered retrospectively—whether the drowned owner, Mr Graunke, still possessed the box in the end or whether it had been stolen from him.

No, say the cells, it is not at all a matter of indifference. Mr Eike was a thief. The property rights of Mr Graunke were violated by Mr Eike and the thief must be punished, even if a lifeboat fishes him out of the water. Even if the owner, Mr Graunke, had no standing to pursue legal steps, which are now of no use to him. Because there is a great difference between being right and getting one's rights. But what is the point of a right that is of no use at all to Herr Graunke who drowned in the icy waters? We all serve no one, said the individual cells. We are not slaves.

Hitler as 'Moonwalker'

A Conversation about Hitler's Character Traits

Ernst Jünger, who was known to be interested in entomology, interviewed the genealogist Charly Scheydt, formerly of the Reich Security Main Office, who is now an entrepreneur in a valley in Baden-Württemberg.

JÜNGER. What if you imagine his face without a moustache?

SCHEYDT. It's a rough but certainly not run-of-the-mill face. It has more Franconian than Austrian features.

JÜNGER. Jewish?

SCHEYDT. Hardly.

JÜNGER. Can you see something like that on the surface?

SCHEYDT. To a very small extent.

JÜNGER. Is there any Asian influence? Or even barbaric?

SCHEYDT. Where is that supposed to come from? You can't judge such matters. The body is veiled. Only the face and hands can reveal such things.

JÜNGER. What if he were Asian?

SCHEYDT. According to our holistic approach, that can't be. The soul always expresses itself through the body. I would say, therefore, no. He is of 'normal' Celtic origin, so to speak, a Westerner or Occidental, someone from the lower middle class or upper lower class with opportunity for advancement (as the son of a father who reached the rank of a civil servant). As long as he doesn't derive his status from his mother at all, a maid who got pregnant out of wedlock and then got married. Status: defender.

JÜNGER. 'You and only you should be the secret of my soul.'

SCHEYDT. It's something that happens quite often. Even if it's in this pure culture and sharpness doesn't happen often. He worked on himself in solitude.

JÜNGER. I don't usually think of you to be so talkative.

SCHEYDT. I also normally don't get asked questions either.

JÜNGER. So you say: The 'disease of the will' as diagnosed by N., which is endemic to the century, must also be evident in the Führer. He can't form a unified will and thus can't make 'irrevocable decisions' (of which he always speaks), because Westerners generally can't do that. In lonely moments, he reflects and that makes his 'will' crumble.

SCHEYDT. You can regard him as a 'model actor of the silent-film era'. Such an artistic 'will', produced in a planned economy, can look the same for ten or twenty years and is independent of the environment. Hitler's sensitivity contradicts this. It 'mirrors' impressions from his surroundings. He hears something yesterday and condenses it into an 'inspiration' the next day.

JÜNGER. Are there examples?

SCHEYDT. 21 February 1943; 28 February 1943; 4 April 1943; 20 April 1943 (four times); 1, 4, 8, and 15 May 1943, just to take snapshots after Stalingrad.

JÜNGER. And you call that 'hunches'?

SCHEYDT. Or instinct. Even though there can be no instinct among Occidentals. A 'lunar type'.

JÜNGER. What does that mean?

SCHEYDT. A moonwalker.

JÜNGER. And means what?

SCHEYDT. He picks up impulses, intones rhythmically. It's quite wrong to associate him with his drawings or architectural interests. He could have become a psychic, or an actor had these professions been considered serious in our Western societies. 'A singer of history'. According to Homer, a 'seer'. In this respect, a hunch or instinct.

JÜNGER. Do you have examples?

SCHEYDT. I counted 7,140.

JÜNGER. What about counter-examples?

SCHEYDT. None.

JÜNGER. What of mistakes?

SCHEYDT. That's something entirely different. A hunch can be deceptive and above all fail. We count mistakes in abundance.

JÜNGER. How many?

SCHEYDT. 417.

JÜNGER. How did you arrive at this level of accuracy?

SCHEYDT. There are unreported cases. I only counted the obvious errors. And of those, only the basic ones. I subtracted recurrences of the same error, otherwise it would be 3,192. As I said, this excludes the number of unreported cases resulting from considerations not properly conveyed like, for example, waking up in the morning or falling asleep at night that were not logged. Or when he was on cross-country trips. Complete overviews of his utterances are only available from 1942 onwards. That is also his worst phase when no one could understand him. You can't understand him at all by measuring data.

JÜNGER. So the figures are illusory then?

SCHEYDT. Of course.

JÜNGER. Let's get to June 1940. The victory over France is achieved. A war against Russia, as predicted in *Mein Kampf*, is by no means decided. Compared with other Western robber societies, the regime is barbaric. It is murderous, for example.

But it is not yet killing peoples. At this point, the Führer is asleep. What can he do?

SCHEYDT. He didn't do it.

JÜNGER. But what was there on the level of possible intuition?

SCHEYDT. A lot.

JÜNGER. A lot of other things?

SCHEYDT. Certainly.

JÜNGER. Did he ever for a moment think of how 'Bismarck was crying in Nikolsburg when the generals went to seize Vienna'?

SCHEYDT. For just a moment. He had a 'decision', brittle like all the others . . .

JÜNGER. Based on what?

SCHEYDT. Based on a simple train of thought. Now that Versailles is rebuffed, fate must not be provoked. Above all, don't lose any tall ships. Reach an arrangement with the British Isles, one of mutual disinterest. Host the 1950 World Exhibition in Berlin. Mars and moon journeys. Space in Africa. Buildings in Linz. Irrigation in the Sahara. Clean up Gibraltar, build a dam there (even though it would be difficult to secure militarily against attacks from the Atlantic). Nordic passage through the fjords. And 360 new Wagner tenors for Middle Franconia alone.

JÜNGER. He could have continued all that?

SCHEYDT. Without a doubt.

JÜNGER. Why did it all fail?

SCHEYDT. Not because he didn't understand a thing about power. He understood or 'intuited' a great deal about this.

JÜNGER. Where did it come from?

SCHEYDT. The moon. He seized it lunarly. He picked it out from an environment, power-hungry and experienced, that didn't understand its own thoughts and feelings.

JÜNGER. In the West, willpower is always nourished by someone else's will.

SCHEYDT. He takes out a 'loan'.

JÜNGER. What then are the rules of power in this case?

SCHEYDT. Such that no added value of it can be retained. Unlike monetary and capital assets, power erodes instantly. I can only hoard it by delaying its use.

JÜNGER. So after the victories over Poland and France, no more showdowns?

SCHEYDT. Just as superstition inspires caution. That brings me to the point that the Führer should have commissioned Martin Heidegger with the intellectual examination of his deeds as early as 1934. In contrast to the supervision on the couch, which is typical of psychoanalysis, a 'dialogue among those standing upright' would have been necessary.

JÜNGER. How utopian!

SCHEYDT. Only as a course of events, but not in the individual details.

JÜNGER. Is this course as brittle as willpower?

SCHEYDT. It's always like that. Like an avalanche of boulders. You can collect each stone separately. They say: for every rock in the hand, there is no avalanche. The individual stones are ground up over the course of time (let's say eleven million years), yielding silicon or possibly humus.

JÜNGER. These aren't timescales for events between 1934 and 1941

SCHEYDT. It's not about time either.

JÜNGER. The 'will' can be ground up in a very short period of time?

SCHEYDT. In fourteen days.

JÜNGER. He's no doubt a lunatic. Toggling between various 'unalterable decisions'.

SCHEYDT. He's not insecure, but he's been inactive for a while. Follow his calendar of events. At the centre of the Reich: nothing for three months, a considerable distance from decisions.

JÜNGER. Consisting of nothing but decisions, orders, studies for attacks.

SCHEYDT. No cities were visited. Because of the threat of assassination. A lunar person needs cities to absorb the energies of others.

JÜNGER. Then the possibility of ending the war was over?

SCHEYDT. It was definitively over. The anti-Hitler coalition was consolidated. Just four months earlier, it was a chimerical entity. A chimera is, for example, the attempt to form a union with France and England.

JÜNGER. Did the Führer understand the failure?

SCHEYDT. Absolutely. From the winter of 1940 onward, he no longer believed that the war could be won.

JÜNGER. Are you sure?

SCHEYDT. Falin researched this.

JÜNGER. Did he commission new studies for attack strategies?

SCHEYDT. Aggressively.

JÜNGER. You see no contradiction therein?

SCHEYDT. Of course not. These are normal contradictions found in all occidental peoples. The rationalization of this means: Frederick the Great also fought in a hopeless situation, but he kept Silesia in the end.

JÜNGER. And then lost in 1945.

SCHEYDT. Hitler didn't care about rationalization, did he?

JÜNGER. What then?

SCHEYDT. He wasn't derived from anything.

JÜNGER. What did he do then?

SCHEYDT. When the matter was hopeless, he began, 'to act without any particular cause'. In other words: he changed his tune. I change the field of employment of power and what I think is right so quickly that something seems to be moving. That is the Hericlitian spirit of silent film.

JÜNGER. And why don't you write a monograph about your theses?

SCHEYDT. For whom?

JÜNGER. Silent film enthusiasts.

SCHEYDT. That's long been replaced by talkies.

JÜNGER. And what is futile, what has become detached, what has become unreal is of no interest to anyone?

SCHEYDT. Nobody in the West.

JÜNGER. Why not?

SCHEYDT. Because no willpower can derive nourishment from it.

JÜNGER. Would it *really* have to remain like that?

SCHEYDT. Like fresh meat.

JÜNGER. Human flesh?

SCHEYDT. Let's not overdo it. You shouldn't talk too much in metaphors.

A Glut of Informers

It was on the *'eve'* of the German Reich's *walk-out* on the League of Nations in Geneva in October 1933. During these hectic days, a serious accusation was made against the undersecretary of the Air Ministry, backed up by the submission of photos of gravestones and documents. Erhard Milch, the undersecretary, was supposed to have a certain proportion of Jewish blood in his veins. The active, hard-working man involved in a thousand ongoing matters saw himself 'caught in the act' like a criminal. The informant, Theo Croneiss, was a high-ranking party member, head of the Air Force–SA[7] and chairman of the Messerschmidt aircraft company. Erhard Milch was *ashamed*, felt himself (although 'innocent') hurt to a degree that later he could never again understand. Never was he so ashamed as in those seven October days when he saw himself exposed as a 'boy one-quarter Jewish'. Not even in 1945 when British commandos took away from him—later he was the field marshal and 'creator' of the Luftwaffe—his marshal's baton and his staff officer's cap and threw them in the dirt. Nor when German fighter planes proved a failure and the Reich fighter plane staff under Engineer Saur took over his responsibilities. Nor in Nürnberg, when he faced the ignominy, which befell the German armed forces through disclosure of the murder of the Jews. He could not foresee the Führer's reaction. Gripped by panic, he went about his daily business. At night he lay in bed bathed in sweat. In whom should he confide?

---

7 The Air Force–SA was of the air section of Hitler's Brownshirts, the mass paramilitary organization of the Nazi Party. Important during Hitler's rise to power, it was emasculated when its leadership was massacred or fled in the 'Night of the Long Knives' in June 1934. This was the army's condition of support for Hitler. [Trans.]

'*Eve*': A metaphysical expression to describe several days or weeks that precede a special event in history or the life of a person. Changes occur, but they can't be interpreted yet. For example, negotiations take place, lively speeches are held. Very rarely is it indeed the 'evening before the event'. A modern battle has, e.g. a preparation time of ten to twenty days. It has no single 'eve'. Thus, too, the dramatic act, by which the German Reich leaves the Assembly of the League of Nations, was an action prepared for months in advance. As an action, it was a propagandistic idea since actual cooperation with the League of Nations had already ceased beforehand. What's more, the League of Nations did not embody any power, but rather an accumulation of older ideas and slogans represented by persons.

Furthermore, 'eve' is no metaphor. Metaphors are mirrors of real experience, which *retard* (like a labyrinth) the facts in question in such a way that the human disposition retains contact with the details of a process moving too fast. The rhetorical figure 'eve', on the other hand, *accelerates* perception (no matter whether it refers to something real or unreal), in that it 'produces' in the form of a *catchphrase* the link to everything that went BEFORE; it is a narrative figure, to which no sunset, dusk, concrete worry or anticipation is ever attached. It is marked, rather, by a flight from reality. Something must be told quickly. To that extent, the foyers of the Air Ministry enlivened by young people, the office corridors, busy hallways, ringing telephones, and anteroom traffic are images which match the term 'eve'. They are the same for weeks on end; anyone, however, who follows this office traffic where the aircraft industries are run will notice distinctions that lie between 'hectic' and 'sleepy'.

Walk-out: The German Reich is a highly abstract federation that also still stands for the opposition contained within it. Indeed, it even includes those departing it in 1933 who still have a German passport. It doesn't walk out on the Geneva residence of the

League of Nations in the form of a group of people like the People of Israel, which really does leave Egypt and set out towards the Holy Land. Rather, the phrase means this: Some foreign ministry officials write papers, which reveal that the German people (or the Reich or its administration or usurpers who have taken possession of the people, the Reich or its administration), humiliated by the dictated Treaty of Versailles, revokes its trust in the League of Nations or confirms that it never placed any trust in this organization in the first place. No doors were slammed, no delegation marches out of the chamber to the hisses of those remaining, no, a statement is issued to the press and simultaneously to an office in Geneva after weeks of passing documents back and forth that were supposed to prevent the drawing-up of this statement.

The feeling of shame: A feeling, 'to sink into the earth'. A threat to one's whole existence and sense of dignity, i.e. to what is unsaleable and, once lost, cannot be retrieved. In fact, shame is not a threat but a loss. If actions follow from this emotional state, then there is a great probability that a human being puts himself in the wrong. As a result, he will have new cause for shame. A shame-guilt spiral arises.

Denunciation: The name Milch is found on gravestones in Silesia, writes Party member Croneiss (enclosure: photos). These gravestones are Jewish. The father of Erhard Milch, as proven by registry office records, was Jewish or half-Jewish. It is unacceptable to the German Air Force–SA that the most senior civil servant of the Air Ministry has Jewish blood in his veins. There follow further observations.

'A powerful man. Suddenly all eyes are averted from him. He has no friends.' To whom can Erhard Milch submit, who can protect him? Should he shoot himself in the head? There can be no retreat from a powerful position like the one he occupies (as an essential member of the imminent re-armament). Could he remain in the Air Ministry as a porter? Could he be in charge of the legal department of a flying school? Could he go back to Lufthansa, all admittedly only with the approval of the Führer?

The linguistic regulation: Erhard Milch races to the places he comes from. A few close friends carry out research on his behalf. Along with Dr Todt, he is considered the most capable technical organizer of the Reich, but not on his own behalf. What will he do wrong? He throws himself into his work, while his trusted friends search records and draw up documents.

The result is the following final report: Before she married the half-Jew Milch, the mother of Erhard Milch yielded to a pure Aryan man. She became pregnant by him. Erhard Milch is an illegitimate child of this union, as is now revealed by the mother's admission, and was only recognized as legitimate by her mixed-blood husband. Thus, in less than a week's time there emerges from shattering investigations a novel about a life that acquits Erhard Milch of the only 'guilt' he could not live with and that he does not wish to explain to the Führer. The latter has read the final report and without comment continues to be in official communication with the undersecretary of the Air Ministry. In December, Erhard Milch is considered saved. He prepares the calculations for the annual balance sheet.

An Assassination by the Cell-Phone Faction

> 'There is some kind of inherent inhibition that prevents him from using his mind, unless it's a matter of things he can see. His mind is completely subjugated by these eyes.'
>
> Manfred Schmidt

Andrej Schmidt, Manfred Schmidt's son, has been a civil servant since 1989 and is a member of the Junior Cell Phone Faction in the Foreign Office, which is about to move to Berlin.

His trousers, jacket, everything always matched. Below his face down, which lacked features that left a lasting impression, he had an athletic body well known in the company of friends for its fast, tireless movement, sexual exploits and socializing. He was popular. He knew the quirks of his superiors. 'He knew how to charm'. Thus, in a few years he had risen from being a business leader's porter in one of the boardrooms to a diplomat in the Foreign Office, abetted by the historic beginning of 1989 that coincided with the beginning of his career. He took a seat when appropriate and he made way for others when that was the right thing to do. He had a lucky touch. Nevertheless, he had worries.

What should he do with his luck? Find himself a match? Not out of love, but rather to possess the fortune of a woman from a wealthy family? Leave state service behind, become a business auditor or, better, a director at one of the big foundations? Where in the world do those movements start spontaneously that, when entrusted, guarantee good fortune? Almost every three months, he had an impulse to try something else. It's a time when an individual can do so much that's wrong because there are so many possibilities. He felt he was in the right place and nevertheless he had worries. Three days had been set aside for Rome. They needed two. He was part of a reconnaissance group. They invaded the hotels straight after landing at the airport, allotted the reserved rooms among one another and made initial contact with the young members of the American delegation. One whole afternoon and evening: the cell-phone faction, twenty-four *members*. They ate, went from one place to the next as if in a daze. Nothing had been properly prepared by headquarters. These days were spent improvising everything.

He sent out invitations six times a year: twice for an asparagus dinner, once for a Frankfurt green-sauce evening, twice for chicken provençale or steaks, once for an Advent or end-of-the-year dinner. Otherwise, he let other people invite *him* to dinner. He is also learning to ride a horse so that he can join the clique that, now transferred to Berlin, has started going out on the weekends to estates in Brandenburg to go riding. Until now he has had to decline, since he can't ride a horse. That's how he lost Franziska von F.

It's urgent that he expand his skills. He isn't blessed with material riches. He can only act for a short time as if he could keep up socially. Thanks to his invitations, his six appointments, he wins 'friends for life'. As with a net: something is caught that can be picked out.

Contacts on the ground in Rome are more difficult. The German delegation knows none of the 'new Americans', those young people, whom Special Envoy Holbrooke hand-picked. Swift contacts 'heated up in the microwave' initially don't produce any friendships, but rather only roles and misunderstandings. Everyone is new here, but they proceed with varying degrees of care. The Americans, who are going on to Budapest and from there to Manila, don't even bother making themselves at home in Rome. They're passing through; they want to wrap things up quickly.

For that, too, he has sufficient skills. He makes elegant proposals to curtail the agenda, but something terrible comes to light: The EU administrator for Mostar, the central figure of the conference, has not been invited. A transportation route is researched. They must get the man, whom no one here knows, in place by the time the meeting begins. Is there a solution that can make this happen?

The five young men from the German delegation take care of such things effortlessly. Agreement with the Americans is perfect before the American Special Envoy, the German Foreign Minister and the heads from Brussels arrive. The agreement is to dispense with one day of negotiations. That means no sortie to Sarajevo, no local session in Mostar, but rather a swift result at the table, a clear decision as to where to go for dinner. Are there any interesting Italian invitations? The young Americans aren't tourists but professionals, interested and brusque. In two days, they want to be introduced to the attractions of Rome, to everything that's hot and important. That's what the young Germans want, too. Thus, an *entente cordiale* is established the evening before. It doesn't have to last long. But perhaps one or another friendship for life will result as well, provided that they meet again. But that's conjecture. These are years when new cadres are formed in the German diplomatic service and likewise in the administration in Washington, a parallel succession of generations is taking place that began in the Federal Republic in 1991 and in the USA in 1992. The cadres, which grow only more insignificant,[8] will together find ways and means of rebuffing latecomers and young people. On this evening here in Rome in a restaurant on the Via Veneto, where they mutually boost one another's egos, they want to go later to a party at Count Giminiano's. A kind of club forms: four young Italians, seven American graduates from Harvard and five young Germans spread around two tables with eight chairs each, sitting together and making friends in something of a rush: as the old men from the diplomatic service of 2026, which they will become one day and already are on their way now. The fatigue from the afternoon has vanished. In just seven hours they feel acclimatized.

His young parents gave him the name Andrej in 1963. In conjunction with the surname Schmidt, the open A (in Andrej) and the choice of the Slavic version of his forename (as opposed to Andreas) reveal what the couple wanted to give their desired child. He has been born into the world with such unfathomable,

---

8 The age is characterized by an explosion of tasks accompanied by a simultaneous reduction in posts. From the civil servant's point of view, the defence of his own post is the issue.

contradictory wishes that he has difficulty orientating himself. He has, therefore, placed his happiness above what we call will. That makes him agreeably lacking in moodiness. Indeed, he can take up the gloomy moods of others and transform them into entertaining conversations.[9]

Now, in the morning, the streets of Rome are crowded. One of the young German diplomats, accompanied by an American, guards the Croatian and Moslem mayors of divided Mostar, who are waiting to be fetched from their hotels. They must be ready for the conference at 11.30 a.m. They should never have been invited, say the Italians. But now they're here. Meanwhile the German Foreign Minister with retinue and Special Envoy Holbrooke fly into the military airport. They must be picked up. Andrej goes in an embassy car to fetch the EU administrator in Mostar and bring him safely to the conference venue. He has no security detail (because of the rush). The administrator speaks very quickly, like no one else today: the silver-tongued Hans Koschnick.[10]

—Who is already there?

—All the delegations, the two mayors, the Croat, the Muslim.

—What is your function? Aside from playing the part of my chaperone at the moment?

—Political Division of the Foreign Ministry. I'm at the disposal of the Foreign Minister.

—Is he already there?

---

9 Parents: Manfred Schmidt, born 21 February 1921; married to Helena, born 14 July 1946.

10 Hans Koschnik (1929–2016), German politician, former mayor of Bremen and member of the Social Democratic Party of Germany. Served as the EU administrator of Mostar from 1994 to 1996. [Trans.]

—He'll probably be stuck in a traffic jam somewhere as we are now.

—Stuck in traffic with his escort? I doubt it. Have you ever been to Yugoslavia?

—Do you mean what's left of Yugoslavia?

—Bosnia, for example?

—No.

—Then what about what's left of Yugoslavia?

—No.

—In Zagreb?

—No.

—Have you looked at the country on the map?

—I haven't studied it.

—Have you seen it?

—I don't look at a map without good reason.

—You can always find a reason.

—Of course.

The man sat very erect in the car, very stiff, very 'determined and prepared'. He made notes on a piece of paper. He was 'not easy to deal with' for Andrej.[11]

During the negotiations, the young men sat along the edges of the conference hall. The squabbling parties from Mostar took up a lot of speaking time. The German delegation found itself in a difficult position. The crucial mistake had already been made when the Americans invited the Croat mayor.[12]

---

11 Andrej thought the older gentleman to be a theorist or a student leader. Why should he investigate where Rump Yugoslavia is when what had to be organized was an international conference in Rome?

12 The Croat mayor of Mostar had had the EU administrator threatened by an armed gang. The conference would have disavowed Koschnik had the terrorist been allowed to sit at the negotiating table.

It would still have been possible to cancel the invitation a couple of days before, at the latest the evening before. The German reconnaissance group spent this evening getting their contacts with the Italians and Americans up and running. At this point in time, the German Foreign Minister was flying over other countries.

Under the given conditions, it made no difference what the result of the conference was: It remained a summit with the participation of a criminal mayor who should have been forced to resign. How was this cardinal error, which shortly afterwards led to the resignation of the EU administrator and the failure of the 'Mostar Model', to be dealt with in an *elegant way*? First of all, through close personal contacts with the American side established during the break in negotiations and, additionally, through a joint presentation to the press. Andrej brought the EU administrator, who sat stubbornly at the table and said nothing, a large glass of Campari. He was rewarded with a cordial smile, which was immediately extinguished as Koschnick turned back to the negotiating table. No one else had seen the smile that changed nothing regarding the catastrophic results.

Once the invitation to the territorial disputants had exhausted the decision-making possibilities—the fact that they were sitting down at the same table was the whole point—the participants had little more to say to one another. They had to wait until the long speeches, replies and absurd proposals for alterations to the text of the agreement that was supposed to regulate free movement in the city of Mostar were ticked off, and the text, which the EU administrator formulated, was partially pushed through, even though everybody in the room had made their contribution to sacrificing him. He sat implacably in his seat.

After a political accident when nothing more can be saved by actions or apologies, there is a kind of ganging up within a group, a makeshift re-establishment of attitudes. These attitudes finally bring down the injured party. The equilibrium in the group requires that the chairmen stand by the wrong decision, that the orderly conduct of business is resumed on the basis of a wrong decision. Thus, Holbrooke and the German Foreign Minister made no further effort to greet or reconcile the EU administrator and squandered the possibility of a German or European Foreign policy because no one among the group of officials filtering the details of the operation had ever seen the places, about which the conference participants were negotiating.

Parallel to the closing speeches and the press work, the protocol for the departures had to be organized. All was lost, but a head start worth a whole day had been won. Flights were changed, addresses exchanged. The young attachés had time for a brief shopping expedition in Rome.

An Unusual Case of Lobbying

It is not the origin of the SLAVE TRADE that is in need of explanation, but the deplorable manner of its repeal. The British public had come under pressure through the abolition of slavery on the French islands in the Caribbean.[13] Philanthropic spirits in London and Scotland voted for a prohibition of the SLAVE TRADE and the *abolishment* of SLAVERY. Pragmatists warned that too rigid a legislation could lead to resentment on the part of the farmers, i.e. the secession of the British Antilles. A

---

13 Abolition ensued from the decree of the French National Assembly, i.e. by law; according to Hegel, such a legal abolition contains a direct negation, which, however, does not yet say anything about the actual execution. The inertia of circumstances, the remoteness of the location far from the Parisian capital meant an enormous difference in effect. On the other hand, the publicity pressure exerted on the active slave trading monarchies in England and Denmark was a huge factor independent of the effectiveness of the decree.

mediating position with regard to the United States, with which Britain was at war, was necessary in all questions of property; no one was conducting an absolute war.

There is a difference, said the fairly pragmatic Duke of Buccleuch, whether it's a question of acquired property or whether the transport of illegal property is obstructed at the borders or on the high seas. The latter is no worse than a customs duty, the former is unconstitutional.

A united lobby swiftly formed. It was paid for by plantation owners, by the captains of the slave ships, by free traders and by ideologues, who said: After the king was beheaded, we shall not stand by and watch property be crucified. Later the united lobby expelled the ships' captains and the slave traffickers from their ranks. It achieved a compromise: the SLAVE TRADE was prohibited, SLAVE HOLDING continued to be guaranteed as an integral part of the order of property and its practice improved (e.g. as to how runaway or abducted slaves were fetched back).

Heiner Müller and 'The Shape of the Worker'

Hercules, says Heiner Müller, was the first in myths to embody the 'figure of the worker'. In a state of confusion imposed by the gods, he kills 'the dearest thing he has' including his children and his wife and then sets the house on fire. Out of his mind, his destructive behaviour is 'horrific'.

He then hired himself out to the tyrant Eurystheus, who—in order to scrap Hercules's identity as a worker, i.e. to profit from him, but in reality, to destroy him—provided him with twelve tasks, all of which were aimed at accomplishing something impossible, or so Eurystheus thought. But Hercules divides these impossibilities into individual steps, armours himself against doubt and pain and accomplishes these 'works' successfully. He even manages, says Heiner Müller, a thirteenth achievement unknown to us.

This is about activities capable of changing objects (including killing and liquidating) directed at infinity. It's about the shape of a 'living machine'; in the last step, this shape is caught in a poison-soaked net that sears its insides. For fear of punishment, no one dares to obey Hercules's command to light the pyre on which he has sat. Who came up with this story, Heiner Müller asks, a tale that takes place long before Prometheus was chained to the rocks of the Caucasus?

As a child, however, Hercules, son of Zeus and Alcmene, was laid on the breast of the sleeping mother goddess Hera. The giant arc of the Milky Way was created either because Hercules was tired of suckling and spilt the remains of Hera's milk while weaning, or because the deceived goddess awoke from her sleep and tore the infant from her breast, thereby spilling milk. Because of this story, the Milky Way bears her name on wintery nights.

Exploring the core of the Milky Way is, however, the work of astronomy. Inge Werdeloff recently found out at the conference of the American Astronomical Society held in Aspen that there is a GRAVITATIONAL TRAP deep inside the Milky Way, which induces the movements of the circling spiral arms and the clouds of heavy neutrinos forming above the halo. This is a gigantic, organic construction, says Dr Inge Werdeloff, and by no means a 'heavenly machine'. Any mechanical interpretation of this heavenly work, she says, is misguided. She heard this in competent lectures.

From her own research, Dr rer. nat. Werdeloff knows (but what does 'her own' mean when one hundred of the rare astronomy spirits must work together to produce research results?) that the mighty gravitational masses, which we call gravitational traps because they draw all matter and energy into themselves as the 'stinginess of the universe' so to speak, are porous. Quantum mechanics proves this. This stinginess, says Dr Werdeloff, shows all the signs of an 'abstract addiction to pleasure'; the gravitational trap releases a substance from all its pores. So that universes come into being again and again, parallel worlds that together show the *veniality of nature* (Goethe). The 'universe as figure of the worker' thus shows no tendencies at all to move from a beginning to infinity or towards an end, but it is divided into diversity and simplicity such that there is always a *countermovement*, a counter-world that accompanies the *appearance*. The deeply frustrated Hercules carries on his shoulders, therefore, the pillars of the world, which must have recently collapsed. And that is why the dead who awaited the collapse of the world near Aachen at the turn of the first millennium are still waiting in vain. It is not a standstill that prevents the end of work, which has been motorized through no fault of one's own.

ME. I didn't understand that.

MÜLLER. It only refers to Hercules as the 'figure of the worker'.

ME. Because in the cosmos one can't speak of guilt?

MÜLLER. Unless it's in the sense of a balance sheet.

ME. And they don't exist because you can't add up quanta?

MÜLLER. I don't understand anything about such things. But once you become one of these dark walls that draws everything towards it—a mighty barrier of darkness—you will see a flash of lightning that escapes the monster. It's forbidden, but it happens.

ME. But would I 'see' that? Because I'm either observing from within the world of a gravity trap or from within the world of lightning? Nobody sees this work, right?

MÜLLER. Then you also don't see what Hercules sucked on and what confused his senses so much that he destroyed 'what he loved the most'.

ME. No, you can't see both at the same time.

MÜLLER. But you know that you've observed it incorrectly if there's just one thing.

A Musical Interlude for Great Singing Machines

A Project by Heiner Müller and Luigi Nono

In the nineteenth century there was still a great deal of improvisation. The classic singing style typical of castrati voices (with their steady calm breath) had been impatiently given up. With that, the pre-eminence of the voice was gone, the singer became part of the orchestra, a 'symphonist'.

Later, to restore the transcendent uniqueness of the symphony, there was a search for brilliant voices and vocal strength. By contrast, Richard Wagner ennobled the 'lay person' who knew how to play music, and the singer with a powerful voice.

In the twentieth century, however, there developed great singing machines, especially in the training establishments of the two superpowers. A voice singing at full throttle could destroy eardrums and even irrevocably destroy the brain with resonances delivered at very short range. A determined voice can kill.

In his table talks, A. Hitler points out how wrong it is to make voice training or the construction of motorways dependent on so-called demand. He had been informed, he said, there were enough Wagner tenors available. But then it had been shown just how great the bottleneck was. Now, in 1942, in the middle of the war it was almost impossible to train enough powerful voices. And that only pertained to Wagner, but it was also necessary to think of the music that would be required after the final victory. What vocal strength would singers have to acquire through training in order to fill the immense memorials to the fallen soldiers in the East with music. He couldn't judge at the moment whether the human voice could also be considered an ultimate weapon, smashing the willpower of the enemy through amplifiers, amplifying, as it were, the effects of the air force and artillery from the spirit of music. He had the impression, however, that the development of humanity, which now separates us from the animal world—but at the same time also from legends and the arts (that once filled the heaven of the gods) as well as chants and storm songs, etc.—, was by no means concluded yet. It was precisely technology that multiplied human will power to an unbelievable extent. He thought very highly of great artists because they could smash a man to pieces with the power of their voices and shatter or corrode a person's brain. Yet this was something they would have never done (even in anger, even out of impassioned acting on stage). To that extent, the Führer said, music was fundamentally gentle.

As a 'Great Tableau' before Act 5 of their *King Lear*, Müller and Nono wrote an 'Interlude for Great Singing Machines'. Strictly speaking, it was no longer music, but rather a parade of technical sounds and noises that accompany rowdy singing focused on maximum effort. A high soprano, said Heiner Müller, who wants to be heard above the thundering drums in Verdi's 'Requiem', inevitably pisses her pants because nobody's abdomen can cope with the high A range and up with a half-full bladder. This produces a smacking, flowing noise when recorded with a microphone attached below the belt. The deep breaths of the baritone in the stretto sequence in Act 2 of 'Rigoletto' resonate 'powerfully'.

During the *Liebestod*, the singer playing Isolde, Hildegard Behrens, was fighting a tickle in her throat. In his Freiburg studio, Nono isolated her breathing pushed upwards by the suppressed coughing in the pauses that her sheer discipline overcomes with the next drawn-out note. In so doing, Nono collects a 'library of vocal achievements'. He handed the material over to Heiner Müller on a cassette. The aim is to organize a movement of these sounds in space and to perform the spatial sound of excessive singing created by the sixty-six choirs of St Mark's Basilica in Venice.

The corresponding text devised by Müller, which does not refer directly to the sounds or the project, could be read during the concert with the aid of a flashlight. The ruins of extreme vocal control were to be staged in Venice and captured on film as in an exhibition or a zoo, in which disabled veterans (all the classic wounds from both world wars) were on display. The film—Müller's texts are added over four loudspeakers—constitutes the 'Great Tableau' that opens Act 5 of *Lear*. The desperate king no longer rules over even a remnant of a kingdom. His empire lies in ruins.

It was said of Harry Kupfer that he designed his Tristan stage sets in such a way that glasses of water for the singers could be adequately hidden. Nono recorded the wheezing breaths and the sounds of water gulped hastily down singers' throats. Neither Müller nor Nono were dull or lazy when they refrained from unnecessary interventions and left the collected sequences of noise as is. The expressiveness lay in the AUTHENTICITY.

Lohengrin in Leningrad

The Premiere of *Lohengrin* in Leningrad on 22 July 1941

The collective behind Leningrad's Kirov Theatre had been rehearsing *Lohengrin* since March. The premiere was to be the highlight of the 1941 summer season and demonstratively convey the theatre's thanks to the working people of the city. The complete opera was to be performed at the premiere using the same version as the very first St Petersburg production; at subsequent visiting performances in provincial cities and in factory canteens at several industrial combines, the intention was to present a pot-pourri, in some cases even without singers, accompanied by the silent dancing of the ballet ensemble. The premiere was to take place in German. It was set for 22 July 1941.

As we know, German troops burst over the Soviet borders in the early hours that day without declaration of war. In the course of the day, motorized troops encircled Soviet border forces. The radio proved to be an essential link between the people of the great Soviet empire.

Lohengrin had been adopted in the programme since last November, the date of Foreign Minister Vyacheslav Molotov's visit to Berlin; the reasons were essentially practical. The theatre had specialists and singers at its disposal. With Verdi, the orchestra would have been underemployed. The chief musical director, a member of the academy, had taken over a seminar at the College of Military Music, the topic of which was the score of *Lohengrin*. Lots of trouble led to decisions on the day of the attack that appeared problematic. Should the premiere of *Lohengrin* be cancelled? The house was sold out.[14]

---

14 A cancellation gives rise to certain difficulties: 95 per cent of the tickets were divided up among different organizations and plant associations and had already been distributed. A hierarchically selected audience had therefore been organized for the premiere. Only a residual number had been sold, in part with a surcharge, or, as it were,

In the theatre, the situation was as follows: Singers and orchestra members appeared punctually at 8 a.m. They heard the latest news first at home and then in the porter's cubby hole by the stage door. Now they were rehearsing the end of the third act: the departure of the swan; the collaboration of the chorus and singers at the Imperial Diet in Brabant; the Imperial Diet sets off practically en bloc for the east in order to overrun the Huns with war.

After a brief discussion, the artists assumed that more than three months of work couldn't be thrown away, no matter what was happening at the country's borders. A historic moment like this couldn't bear wasting resources. They were less concerned with the 'content' of Richard Wagner's work than with the staging, acting and musical difficulties, which still had to be overcome like a mountain of rubble to be cleared away within a short period of time. At the same time, however, there is also a mountain of pride contained in such work: the pride of the producers.

The director of the opera house calls the First Secretary Antonov of the municipal district.

—Comrade Antonov, we are filled with dismay at the misfortune that has befallen our country.

—Not quite right, Comrade Opera Director, a misfortune will befall the intruders. That's the way it must be passed on. 'They have started something, the end of which they can't foresee.'

—You see things optimistically?

—Absolutely. I don't have any more information either.

—This evening is the premiere of *Lohengrin*.

---

disappeared onto the black market. The management of the Kirov Theatre was attached to the idea that one must honestly be able to retrieve the tickets if a 'full house' were cancelled.

—I know. I'm coming.

—I'm asking because it's a German piece sung in German.

—We've not been attacked by Germans, but rather by fascists and militarists who are oppressing their own people. That's how it must be passed on. That could be clarified by an address before the beginning of the performance. A kind of orientation.

—The opera is sung in German, something that can be interpreted as a provocation if one analyses the texts more closely.

—Given the extremely critical situation, could one perhaps have the singing done in Russian?

—Out of the question. The singers have rehearsed in German.

—They must rehearse again.

—That's impossible in one day. We first must prepare piano scores with Russian text, etc.

—Place Russian-language announcers at the sides of the stage or in the auditorium and present the text in Russian. Could the singers sing somewhat unclearly?

—From the point of view of the general artistic impression, I would advise against that.

—But it would be interesting and informative.

—But also dangerous, given the quality of the texts measured according to their content, Comrade First Secretary.

—Or one leaves out the singing?

—That would be an unusual solution.

—A symphonic performance with spoken text and banners, which can be understood without setting off a brawl. It would be a kind of contemplative evening, a patriotic ceremony.

—How unusual.

—We are living on an unusual day, Comrade. The *1812 Overture* by Tchaikovsky is also without singing and fits very well.

—Comrade Antonov, do you know *Lohengrin*?

—No.

—It is a knight's opera with a supernatural hero. It's about the fantasies of a young Teutonic woman. At the end, there's a kind of party congress of the German knights chaired by their Emperor. Chorus, singers and orchestra are deployed as a collective and are actually inseparable. Translated into Russian, the provocative passages are even more evident than if sung in a foreign language. Italian and Turkish costumes that we have in the wardrobe for the 'Barber of Baghdad' would be best. But that can't be managed by 8 p.m. this evening.

The director of the opera collective was new to his post. He had not been involved in the programming decisions in November 1940. He had no intention of risking his career because of a lack of political instinct. He had recently been transferred here from Alma Ata and was actually designated for a career in the party. Thus, he was concerned to make a value-free report and to *share* responsibility with the political leadership in Leningrad.

The First Secretary responded:

—Would you say it's a socialist piece?

—No.

—Should Richard Wagner be described as a fascist?

—No.

—As a class-conscious bourgeois or a revolutionary?

—In his youth.

—Is there a clear difference between Hitler and Richard Wagner?

—A generational difference.

—Will the opera still be comprehensible if it's cut in half or shortened?

—It's not comprehensible in the strict sense.

—Does it have more *beautiful* music?

—Beautiful music, 'unearthly'.

—You'll have to improvise.

—(The opera director keeps silent.)

The Party Secretary promised to call back in twenty minutes.

At party headquarters in Leningrad that day, everything was done in a rush. Mobilization plans had to be implemented; inventories overdue for months moved to the top of the list of priorities. Then there were phone calls from Moscow, even to the middle-ranking leadership. Most of the time was spent trying to contact the border and the Baltic republics (taking alternate routing via the military communications network, the adjacent networks of the NKVD). Everyone wanted to find out about the situation. None of those responsible had the nerve to attend *Lohengrin*. But all were set to meet at the opera in the evening. Extraordinary moments have a need for inertia; so meals continue to be served and appointments make up the structure of the day.

The tram cars travelled relentlessly along their tracks. The sun moved across the firmament at something of an angle; the museums opened; the factories were restless. Nervousness. Sensuous perception of the situation, which will strangle the life of the city within twelve weeks, was immediately put in its place by 'party attitude'. The political cadres wore the mask of 'iron calm'. Agitated were the hearts and ears 'thinking along' with the wireless sets.

A few minutes of exchanges with officials hurrying past in the corridors of the party headquarters (an office building with a lift) were available to Antonov and served as the basis of a decision. There were various positions.

1. Proposal: Put censors to work to cut the provocative passages from the opera.
2. Proposal: Perform everything as it has been rehearsed.
3. Cancel the opera and perform a repeat of Rimsky-Korsakov with addresses before and after. Possibly start earlier. Pioneer choirs.
4. Proposal: Cancel the opera, but not because of the content, but because of the danger of an air raid. How is the audience, a mass event, to be accommodated in the cellars if there is a German attack at night?

The practically omnipotent dictator of the city, Comrade Zhdanov, knew *Lohengrin*. Antonov walked up a couple of the steps to the main entrance to stand beside him. Zhdanov was hurrying to the Commander-in-Chief of the Northern Armed Forces.

Zhdanov's comments on proposal no. 1: Never 'show influence'. Display 'collective self-confidence'. Performance is the essence of the theatre.

On proposal no. 2: Leningrad is not fighting against Germany, but rather against the fascist aggressors who, first of all, subjugated Germany; they are, therefore, a predatory horde facing their own destruction. 'We don't even acknowledge it as war.'

On proposal no 3: Is *Lohengrin* about a predatory horde? No, not at all. What, therefore, is the position of 'collective Soviet self-confidence': It's precisely on this day that we shall perform *Lohengrin* in German. You ask whether it can be broadcast. It will confuse the enemy if German voices ring out from the Soviet Union's wireless sets.

To Antonov, Leningrad's boss seemed 'drunk with haste'. Neglected Five-Year Plans were to be made good in a matter of days. Antonov had nothing but these words left floating in the stairwell, without a memo, without witnesses. After this ORIENTATION, his doubts were, if anything, greater in size.

In the early evening, the network of Leningrad's hierarchies gathered together in the opera's foyer. Field telephones had been laid for the party leaders and, indeed, as the audience took their seats, they saw the party cadres telephoning, discussing in and around the auditorium, a coming and going that reached well into the loges.

Seven speakers had been distributed around the orchestra. They had megaphones. Each standing at a lectern, they read Wagner's texts and stage directions in Russian in synchrony with the music. There were three female prompters and four actors chosen from the theatre company whose dark and bright voices seemed to match the characterization of Ortrud, Elsa, Lohengrin, Heinrich I and Telramund. The speakers were instructed to whisper loudly.[15]

The backdrop for the first and last acts was changed. Decor from the 1st of May ceremonies had been brought from props and the back of the stage was rigged out with flags and topical slogans. To reduce the risk that could result from an air raid, the 'private' second act was omitted. In a vague sense, the first and third acts produced a 'more political' version of the opera. The abridgment 'condensed' the opera into a 'demonstration of Leningrad's will to survive'. That is what was announced.

Antonov, who had saved the evening, was hearing the music for the first time in his life. He was already won over during the prelude and congratulated himself on the idea of having members of the ballet lay flowers in front of the flags and posters with

---

15 The loud whispering was suitably amplified by the megaphones. It turned out that whispered text prevails over singers and orchestra and is less disruptive coming out of the middle of the audience in the orchestra than 'actorly speech'. Whispering gets rid of the traces of theatrical training as well as of the realism of everyday language. Both are advantageous for the peculiarity of the Wagner's texts.

slogans before the chorus and singers entered. The languid, yet gentle pace of the strings and the pattering of the ballet shoes on stage seemed to him expressive of a 'functioning realistic partisanship'. An appropriate evening for the beginning of a war that no one here had wanted. He found the speaking voices enhanced by megaphones splendid, as they inserted scraps of words between the music and the singing so that listeners always had something vague to think about; this vagueness, Antonov thought, became filled with the events of the day such that scraps of memories from the radio broadcasts of powerful marches and songs also entered into Richard Wagner's music. The audience, essentially plant employees, party members, but also a few members of the military, appeared both happy and comforted to be together.

That same night, the members of the orchestra were armed as a special unit and marched off to the front. The opera was closed. Within an hour, everything not directly necessary for battle was cancelled. Socialist generosity, such as Antonov had in mind up to the beginning of the opera ('magnanimity as an intellectual weapon'), was over and done with. To Antonov, it seemed, however, a sign of future victory that the war doesn't immediately divide everyone and everything into friend and foe, but that at least for a short time, i.e. for one day, an exceptional capacity for differentiation could be worked out. That came to life for one evening: a space between aggression and art.

Twilight of the Gods in Vienna

(for Heiner Müller)

'The way the twentieth century appropriates music.'

Gerard Schlesinger, *Cahiers du Cinéma*

'Whatever is not broken cannot be saved.'

H. Müller, *Cruel Beauty of an Opera Recording*

In March 1945, the metropolis of Vienna was surrounded by Soviet shock troops. Only to the north and northwest was there still a land link to the Reich. At this moment, the Gauleiter and Reich Defence Commissar Baldur von Schirach, ruler of the city, ordered a final gala performance of *Twilight of the Gods*. In the hopeless situation of the city and the Reich, the despair of the Nibelungs (but also the hope of return contained in the final chords) composed by Richard Wagner was to be broadcast on all southeast transmitters, as long as these were still in German hands. 'Even if the Reich is destroyed, music must remain with us.' The opera house, shut down, bolted and barred on all sides since October, was opened again. Orchestra members were brought in from the fronts to the capital of the administrative district. On the evening before the dress rehearsal (including the orchestra and costumes but not the third act when Valhalla is in flames, the final rehearsal was then to be recorded and broadcast by the radio station, a premiere was dispensed with), US squadrons flying from Italy to Vienna bombed the city centre. THE OPERA BURNED DOWN.

Now the opera rehearsed in groups split up between various air-raid shelters throughout the city. The left side of the orchestra worked in five groups in cellars on Ringstraße; the right side, including timpani, in four cellars on Kärntner Straße as well as on side streets. The singers were distributed among the orchestra groups. They should try singing 'like instruments'. They could not be positioned in relation to one another since they were singing in different cellars after all. The conductor sat in the wine cellar of a restaurant, at first without any connection, but was soon linked to all the cellars by a FIELD TELEPHONE.

Artillery shells exploded in the vicinity. During rehearsals, there were two daylight raids by units from the US Air Force. Defending heavy artillery dug in nearby and zeroed in on Soviet long-range artillery. Infantrymen and railway workers had been allocated as runners for the rehearsing music sections. The news they delivered was supplemented by field telephones that not only linked the conductor with the orchestra sections but also linked them with one another. The sound of the rehearsing neighbours produced via the dedicated line was amplified in each case by loudspeaker. Thus, the musicians in one shelter could register the broad outlines of the musicians' sounds playing in another far away, while they themselves rehearsed the parts of the score for which they were responsible. Later the conductor hurried from cellar to cellar and gave instructions on the spot. THERE ARE COMPLETELY DIFFERENT CONSIDERATIONS TO BE TAKEN INTO ACCOUNT, HE SAID, THAN THOSE AT A DRESS REHEARSAL WHERE EVERYONE IS PRESENT.

A different sound was produced. The noise of the final battle for Vienna could not be filtered out and the orchestra fragments produced no unified sound. Since Vienna's bridges were under threat, the commanding officer, Colonel General Rendulic passed on a warning to the staff of the Reich Defence Commissar. The evacuation of the singers and orchestra members to the west of Austria must be pushed up if they were to be saved. Consequently, it was impossible to wait for the dress rehearsal. Instead, something had to be improvised. As a result, the Reich Defence Commissar, a still-young man, ordered that the radio recordings of the sound worked out thus far were to be made immediately, i.e. that very same day. The radio engineers began to record, therefore, the 'fragments' of *Twilight of the Gods* at 11.30 a.m. with the first scene from the third act (Siegfried and the Rhine maidens).

The orchestra played up to the end of the third scene of the third act. Acts one and two of the music drama were to follow. The intention was to patch it all together at the radio station, or instead, once the original tapes had been flown out of Vienna, to fit everything together and broadcast the work without interruption from the Reich's broadcasting station in Salzburg.

BY CHANCE, however, 3,000 meters of 35 mm Agfa colour film stock were stored in Vienna. Lieutenant Colonel of the Staff Gerd Jänicke, who consolidated the four propaganda companies under his command in the besieged area around Vienna, had the firm intention of filming the tragedy of this city. Now his decision took solid shape. He ordered the orchestra's achievements to be captured on film and in sound, and without consideration of the camera's own noise, since a camera blimp[16] was not available. To Jänicke, the shooting of the last act of *Twilight of the Gods* seemed the crowning conclusion to his seven years of devoted work as chronicler and propagandist. There was nothing to be glossed over. Perseverance was to be documented. Put on record would be what would not perish with the German Reich: German music.

The third act and parts of the first were recorded with five cameras, each with connected recording equipment. Anti-aircraft searchlights were used for lighting: they shone on the cellar walls and gave a bright, indirect light. For the complete impression, robust improvisation was necessary: thus, those singers and orchestra sections in other cellars not recorded by the film teams were patched through to the performance via radio telephone

---

16 A protective soundproof casing that muffles the loud sound of the camera's motor.

and stored on 17.5 mm perforated magnetic tape; later they were added to the mix. In the first scene of the third act, an effort had still been made to achieve an overall sound, but after that there was a shift to presenting the fragments in the second and third scenes to the listeners one after the other. In the film, these scenes were heard and seen nine times in succession: each time, a noisy section of the orchestra plays the score that was being rehearsed in the cellar in question.

The civilian management of Radio Salzburg displayed the institutional cowardice typical of broadcasting corporations. It concluded that the sound recording of *Twilight of the Gods*, assembled from a number of unequal parts, could not be broadcast for 'qualitative reasons'. Telephone calls from the staff of the Reich Defence Commissar were unable to persuade it to alter its judgement. As if in the Reich's present situation what matters most is a high-fidelity recording typical of peacetime! said Captain von Tuscheck, the officer on Schirach's staff responsible for the operation. But the civilian management in Salzburg remained adamant. It transmitted a pre-recorded version of the third act of *Twilight of the Gods* and after that only marches until the surrender of Salzburg.

Lieutenant-Colonel Jänicke's propaganda units, on the other hand, safeguarded the undeveloped negative and sound recordings in a garage in Vienna's Hofburg Palace. The intention was to transport them to Oslo or Narvik on one of the last aircraft flying out of Vienna. There was a film laboratory in the north. The enemy was to be deprived of the recording by presenting a last message from the fighting Reich. Unlike 1918, bodies, tanks and entire cities were smashed in this war; the spirit, however, remained intact. Theoretically, said Jänicke, final victory is possible, even if all means of defence were destroyed, through will and intellectual weapons alone. This was true, above all, for the medium of music.

The transport of the *Twilight of the Gods* film could no longer happen because no vehicles were available to deliver it to the airport.

Meanwhile, night had fallen. The musicians climbed out of their cellars and into the open air. Infantry NCOs led them through the city centre, which was under unsighted artillery fire. They reached buses and were driven out of Vienna (the last ones out of the closing pocket). In the morning, they found themselves in rural surroundings. They were distributed among farms in the neighbourhood of Linz and a few days later arrested by American troops.

The cans of film in the garage, still properly labelled, were secured by Soviet officers and forgotten. A Georgian colonel who spoke French handed the stack of reels over to a Tartar lieutenant-colonel who could read the German writing (which admittedly he only revealed to trustworthy friends and not the Georgian colleague). The lieutenant-colonel had the undeveloped film material brought to his garrison town, Sochi, where it was stored in the basement of the municipal museum for decades.

In 1991, after the collapse of the imperium, a young composer, who described himself as Luigi Nono's representative for Russia, discovered the film stock. He followed a lead published in a music periodical for specialists based in the Crimea, the issues of which can be called up on the Internet on a single browser window. Without ever having seen any of the materials or even being familiar with the place where it was stored, the young man organized the transfer of the film to a studio in Hungary, where he had the material developed. The rolls of positive film were then brought to Venice. The intention was to present the soundtrack in St Mark's Cathedral on the tenth anniversary of Luigi Nono's death.

A film editor and female assistant to J.-L. Godard, who learned about the discovery, insisted on being allowed to process the materials in the laboratories of the Cinétype Studios in Paris and showed a group of staff members from *Cahiers du Cinéma* and the *Cinémathèque* the 3,000 metres of film in sound and vision.[17]

The effect of the material (after fifty years storage) was 'enchanting', writes Gerard Schlesinger of *Cahiers du Cinéma.*

The 35 mm film stock had first been developed and showed signs of light exposure and discolouration; subsequent processing of the unexposed negatives in the lab revealed superimposed shadows and echoes. Parts of the material are scratched and acquire, contrary to one of Walter Benjamin's theses, a *unique* characteristic because of the damage. 'The soundtrack,' writes Schlesinger, 'displays a "cruel beauty" or "something like strength of character"'. Richard Wagner should *always* be 'fragmented' in this way. Authentic sounds of the camera and the artillery and bomb detonations can also be heard. This field recording, the 'being-in-the-middle-of-it-all', puts a rhythm to Wagner's music and turns it from a phrase of the nineteenth century into the PROPERTY of the twentieth.

In some images, the camera and the tripod as well as the sound apparatus are visible. The 'interventions of the female prompters have the high tone colour of Ufa sound films. The high pitch of the voices in the sound films of the time appears, therefore, to be a result of not only the actors' speech training but also the rules of the sound recording.'

It would be a mistake, according to Schlesinger, to mix the sound fragments. Unlike the original recording, that would result

---

17 Processing = image and sound matched on the editing table. She edited the 17.5 mm perforated tapes, along with their curious sound fragments, into a coherent version. Otherwise, it would not have been possible to synchronize the image sections and the much longer sound sections, she said. She had followed the descriptions noted on the tins with the sound tapes. She didn't speak any German herself, but had an acquaintance at Goethe-Institut Paris, with whom she occasionally slept.

in a POOR OVERALL SOUND. The mixing of the sound sections only documented the *intention* of those shooting the film, not, however, what they *did*: Here, it was a matter of an ingenious discovery, that is, the BEAUTY OF FRAGMENTS.

Thanks to the intervention of *Cahiers du Cinéma*, the three-thousand metres of film and the surplus sound fragments are consequently shown as a total of 102 separate pieces. Each picture section has been allocated only one soundtrack. Where pictures are missing, a concert without images is heard in the cinema. At the suggestion of *Cahiers du Cinéma*, Nono's representative included the work in the composer's catalogue. A successful work is not what an individual mind thinks up as a score, but whatever treasures of music he finds and preserves. Indeed, it is an art getting hold of such treasures. I wouldn't have ever been able to think up a telephone booth voice, says Nono's representative, not least one possessing such powers of expression. This is work of sound and vision work from the twentieth century is unique. 'Property is the luck of finding such once-in-a-lifetime treasures.'

Description of a Picture

They were sitting at the back of the projection room in the labs of the Cinétype Studios in Paris. They were supposed to collaborate on logging the patterns of combined sounds and images. It was a matter of quality control.

—You can see the light bulbs shining on the cellar ceiling and torches shining on the music stands.

—Apart from that, the walls are bright.

—The torches are replaced from time to time.

—And when the batteries have to be changed. You can see that some of the torches are already growing weaker.

—The faces are in the shadows.

—Yes, but the forceful movement of the musicians moves the shadows so that something 'spiritual' keeps the room in motion, an indication of the 'industrious figures'.

—Clouds of dust floating past the lamps. Those are shells exploding.

—Or bombs.

—Yes.

—The dust has to be wiped from the instruments. More often than at rehearsals at the opera. Look here: The brass players take a break to clean their instruments. Mixed dust and spittle.

—Now this group has to jump to bar 486?

—Exactly. So now it's synchronous with the strings and the solo soprano again, whom we hear, amplified by loudspeaker, from the neighbouring cellar via the radio telephone.

—Would you say it sounds 'raspy'.

—It's simply how a piece of German army communications equipment sounds. Listen, the artillery also sounds tinny in the recording, i.e. in terms of sound quality it's a mistake.

—Here, three of the seven orchestra sections lose track of one another.

—Just like in the churches of the High Middle Ages. The notes wander around in space. There's no 'consonance'.

—But with the best will in the world it's impossible to say that the radio telephones, and here you see only one telephone connection with loudspeakers directly linked by wire, produce a *qualified space*. In this case, it's more like an anti-cathedral.

—But the imagination of a space works all the better.

—Why better?

—Think of the actual situation. At any moment one of the other musicians' cellars (or one's own) can be hit and collapse. Then you'd only hear the sound of the catastrophe. The actual situation determines the imagination.

—So it's not the sound of a space, but rather of a cage?

—Of course: the group sound of many spaces. A kind of *Lebensraum*. At last, music has for once arrived in real conditions. That's achieved not by a symphony orchestra setting up in a factory and acting as if that's a place for concerts. The factory is made unreal and that's not a way for making music real. Here, however, in the emergency of besieged Vienna, there arises a new kind of sound space of real music: the resurrection of music out of the spirit of history. The spaces are the message. In the rattle of musical notes I imagine the starry sky. Something pure, something clear.

—And you think Richard Wagner had that in mind?

—That's what I assume.

—But he doesn't belong to the twentieth century.

—A timeless genius is used to picking up everything musically valuable. Do you hear that? That's brass group 4 with a kettledrum and three cellos from the right-hand side of the orchestra. It sounds very much like *The Jewess*, Act 5, Scene 1. Wagner found his inspiration *there*, and here it returns to the right space: back to Meyerbeer. Music cannot be expropriated.

—It sounds 'interesting'.

—'Captivating'. That's the right word.

—It's dark here.

—Yes, a series of near hits has destroyed the electric cable. Some of the torches are lying on the floor. Look, infantrymen running up the cellar stairs to repair the electrical connections. You can see something with the help of the pocket lamps, which are now being attached to the music stands again. And there, candlelight, a candelabra with twelve candles used to light the room. It's useless for individual musicians to read notes but comforting for the room as a whole. There's the conductor coming in. He whispers instructions to the first violinist and to the two singers. He's carrying a basket with twelve new torches and provisions.

—The other cellars know nothing about the temporary loss of this group of musicians?

—They do. They're told by radio. On the left there you see an army radio operator. There are also female prompters distributed between the cellars. This one here has a Hungarian accent and has been borrowed from the operetta.

—Would it not have been a better idea to play *Rheingold* rather than *Twilight of the Gods*? It would have been a hopeful beginning. Better from the point of view of propaganda than a drama of doom.

—The people in Vienna were no longer prone to exaggeration and couldn't lie any more either. The people who organized this were desperate and full of grief.

—Is it an unconscious work of art with a claim to truth?

—To the extent that every intention came to nothing, and that something else was produced, something no one person wanted. No one ever imagined that air-raid shelters could become workshops for art.

—It's difficult to believe.

—It's quite a find. The main achievement consisted in finding this in the cellars of the Sochi Museum.

—Do you think there are many more such finds to be made in the world?

—There are many more. You have to assume that for 6,000 years now something is always lying hidden somewhere or has been lost.

For one man to kiss another on both cheeks has been suspect ever since the arrest of Christ; it has become suspect once more because of the Socialist fraternal kiss, especially after the kisses were followed by betrayal and collapse of the imperium.

Even before cancer could kill him, Heiner Müller was killed by kisses on his (badly shaven, gaunt, already underfed) cheeks. A mass of viruses collected before Christmas was transferred by a touch to the skin of his cheek. A current of air—theatre air—carried the deadly germs towards the dramatist's mouth and nostrils. This happened after the rather unsuccessful premiere of his play *PHILOCTETES*, on one of the evenings between Christmas and New Year in the year 1995.

PHILOCTETES has been marooned on an island by his travelling companions. He is said to be dying. He's so badly injured that it no longer seems worth taking him along. To lose one's companions, with whom one once set out into the world full of hope, and then to be left behind alone, unable to communicate—according to Sophocles, that is the highest form of tragedy; as far as heroes (and not cities), the destruction of nations and whole families are concerned.

The fate of PHILOCTETES—broken up into speeches and responses, monologues and intermissions—did not move his friends from Prenzlauer Berg. For Müller, too, it was by no means the case that he felt himself abandoned by friends (he was gradually abandoned by his enemies, the informers grew tired of denouncing him, since he evidently answered all accusations by saying that he carried on writing under the time pressure of his incurable illness, the pressure of the pain, more intensively than ever). A superfluous drama. A waste of time for the audience? For the theatre director? Depends on what waste means.

During these days, Müller was unaccompanied at certain hours. He could no longer pull himself together sufficiently to refuse or break off a conversation. An intern from the *Berliner Zeitung*, which at that time was rapidly attracting people one after the other and distributing them between posts as part of its effort to grow the newspaper for the new capital, sat down beside the starving Müller, took a tape recorder from his carrier bag and began to question him:

TRAINEE. Herr Müller, you cannot have failed to notice that the applause at the end—it was already long past midnight—was sparse.

MÜLLER. (*no response*)

TRAINEE. Don't you want to say anything about that?

MÜLLER. No.

TRAINEE. But an evening like that must have disappointed you as theatre director.

MÜLLER. (*raspy*): What makes you think that theatre has to be interesting?

TRAINEE. Because of the taxpayers' money used up for it.

MÜLLER. So because of the miserliness of government funding? Miserliness is a poor adviser.

TRAINEE. What would be a better one? Could you explain that by taking *PHILOCTETES* as an example?

MÜLLER. I can't explain anything.

TRAINEE. Or maybe suggest one?

MÜLLER. There's a considerable distance.

TRAINEE. Distance from what?

MÜLLER. From a hero of antiquity.

TRAINEE. A tragedy of remoteness?

MÜLLER. (*no response*)

Meatballs are brought; they are unsuitable for the dramatist's damaged oesophagus. With mixed feelings, which he took to be hunger, Müller sat in front of the plates. His feeling urged him to change something about his momentary condition; no condition could be worse. Lethargically, he threw himself into the conversation once more. Any other measure to change his state would have been more agonizing.

MÜLLER. The comrades depart for Troy. The town is taken by cunning and burnt. PHILOCTETES is wounded. He's a burden on his comrades. In the Second World War, he would have been shot so that he didn't suffer. His companions, fearful of the gods, leave him behind on the island with a small quantity of provisions but without valuable weapons (that would have been a waste). A first-class opportunity for thinking. For the first time in this hero's life, PHILOCTETES thinks something. It is not anything hopeful.

TRAINEE. In my desperation—it's about three hours of an evening after all—my eyes wandered from side to side of the rectangular stage. My eyes were not captivated by anything on the set. Naked men, reciting texts.

MÜLLER. And why didn't you close your eyes? You have to get to Greece somehow. Theatre is something that throws back echoes. If you don't transmit anything, then the stage doesn't throw anything back. Try it some time with your eyes shut.

TRAINEE. Interesting advice.

MÜLLER. I only give interesting advice. But that is not the function of theatre. The function of the theatre is: to waste time. So that time passes so that your eyes shut. At some point, the end of the day must come. The function of theatre is to set the keystone in place for that.

He reached for a beer mat and wrote something on it.

TRAINEE. What's that? Can I keep it? A Müller text?

MÜLLER. I find it hard to go on talking. Let's stop.

He gave the young man the beer mat with his autograph. The dramatist had written: 'There is no route, neither by sea nor by land, to the Hyperboreans'.

The tall interviewer with a bright future, who had helped Müller bridge a terrible hour of waiting for the predictably late or even impossible way home and the onset of sleep by simply talking (given that he couldn't eat anything nor fill up with any drinks any more), was pleased about his haul.[18]

He secured an original interview and an original autograph, which would surely appreciate in value. He interpreted Müller's words like this: theatre is an extravagant enterprise.

Müller had wanted to say something else: There is a borderline between REAL and UNREAL. Gods once landed at such points on the planet. Neither the paths of the imagination nor any travelling leads to them if one does not unwaveringly gaze at the rectangular stage and make one's eyes empty until they see nothing any more and nothing more happens except that time passes. THAT IS THE FUNCTION OF THEATRE. In those days Müller had difficulty speaking at all. Substantial parts of his stomach had been pulled up to his throat and sewn on there as a substitute for his oesophagus. How nice that in the theatre members of the audience are able to discover their generosity. In fact, they only succeed in doing so in failed productions. It's an operation against the miserliness of life, while the river of life flows by.

---

18 Cousin of Andrej Schmidt, but, because his mother didn't particularly love him, eccentric.

The Death of the Gods —
A Black Hole at the Heart of Rome

> 'Modern men, blunted with respect to all Christian nomenclature, can no longer understand the spine-chilling superlative, which for the taste of the ancient world lay in the 'paradox God on the cross'. There has never since been a comparable boldness in the act of reversal, anything equally awful, questioning and dubious as this formula: It promised a revision of all the values of antiquity.'

Great upheavals, moments of desperation come in droves. At the same time as the one god was nailed to the cross on Golgotha, fanatics near Corinth denounced a cheerful, cute Greek god, who thought he was Mercury. He was brought before the governor and on a hillside a few stadia from the city, already in the interior of the Peloponnese, he was fastened to the cross; to his followers, it was quite an incomprehensible death.

The centurion charged with carrying out the execution, an adherent of the sun cult (the majority of legions were followers who worshiped the central heavenly body), writes Heiner Müller, was disturbed by the puzzling action and the news of further sacrifices of gods in Northern Epirus. In an address to his men, he said: Everything that we do has now become meaningless since, without gods, we do not exist. These gods are being killed in a fit of madness by religious groups. We soldiers are appointed to carry out the execution. If we acquiesce—and what else should we soldiers do except obey the orders of our superiors?—then it's no longer worth living on earth. We are 'de-materialized' (*derealisati sumus*).

Should we march on Rome then? Massacre the lawmakers? Should we change emperors?

At this point, applause interrupted the commander's speech. The legionaries beat their shields and removed their helmets. In this extreme emergency, they were ready to declare the centurion imperator and advance on the nearest provincial capital.

Under Emperors Vespasian and Titus, such a revolt was condemned to failure. The legionaries were surrounded. After they had been drawn up for the last time, every tenth man was handed over to the executioner, the rest sold into slavery. In accordance with the conventions of war, the centurion, who had commanded the mutineers, was crucified. Afterwards, the judgement handed down by the Corinthian praetor with respect to the cheerful Greek god as well as eighty-five other judgements, which had been imposed in the provinces on the grounds that someone had described himself as a god, were quashed by the Senate. In those days, the cohesion of heathen antiquity crumbled.

At first, no one noticed the vacuum, which had come into being at the heart of the Empire and consumed all virtue and ultimately also the will to maintain such an Empire. The empty place in the heavens (i.e. in the breast of every man, as long as gods rule) is occupied by dangerous monsters, delusions, exaggerations. That's because gods, once crucified, cannot be resuscitated. The empty space inside us, writes Ephimarchus (an educated slave), is immediately filled by hostile powers because men cannot bear any emptiness in their breast.

A Forecast for the Year 2007

How in 1946 the European Idea Was Realized on a Railroad

Almost all the great civilizing achievements in the area of railroad systems are to be found at their most perfect pitch only in the colonies. Indian, South African, Chinese locomotives constitute the top class of robust and PHYSICALLY BEAUTIFUL

SYSTEMS, which out of various considerations could not be fully developed in the centres of European industry.

In 1946, the administration of the French State Railways was represented by officers on the staff of the French army occupying Germany and Austria. At their disposal (the country was run like a colony) were engines and carriages of the Orient Express Company, an enterprise which had provided a connection from Paris to Istanbul since the turn of the century; the connection had been repeatedly broken by the Balkan wars and the outbreak of two world wars. Without these interruptions, said Commandant F. Brissot of the 6th Cavalry Regiment in Tübingen (he had long ago stopped riding horses), it would have been normal to go by train from Paris to Baghdad; at some point in time, one could have reached Bushir on the Persian Gulf.

The military administration first repaired the stretch from Überlingen to Lindau. Four carriages, two dining cars, two engines; hand-picked staff. Lindau had been annexed to the French Zone of Occupation as an unaffiliated county town so that there was a corridor linking the French Zone in southern Germany and the French Zone in Austria.

The train, which under French command was *intended* as an experiment to travel the entire stretch via Vienna, Belgrade, Salonica to Istanbul, Ankara, Erzerum (and from there to Tiflis), was halted at a Soviet checkpoint south of Vienna.

Under the conditions of 1946, Brissot wrote to the Prime Minister of the French Republic: It is essential for overall French interests that we restore the link from Paris to Serbia, which would have been so important in 1914. Demand, flow of traffic, frequency? The question, says Brissot, cannot be posed like that. It may be assumed, however, that as soon as rail services were established crowds of intellectuals who always tended to move from east to west would flow towards France; the other way around, adventurers, makers of plans and commercial travellers would fan out towards the Balkans and the Near East and benefit France in turn. But in any case, concluded Brissot, it was important for the standing of the French occupying power (this was hardly taken into account by Western Allies and ignored by the Soviet occupying power) to undertake something CONSPICUOUS.

At first, as already mentioned, the transport project was only realized between Überlingen and Lindau. Seven times a day as a kind of Lake Constance connection one of the engines and some carriages travelled back and forth. The dining car offered vol-au-vents, cakes, liqueurs, French cooking and on Wednesdays Turkish cooking. If the French authorities had to entertain envoys of the British or American Zone, then for lunch the one-hour trip in one of the saloon cars was chosen.

After Brissot's transfer to the Foreign Ministry in Paris, the undertaking was abandoned in the harsh winter of 1946–47. In order to found Europe, Brissot reported from Paris, several such transversals are needed, of which this, crossing the continent to the southeast, will be the first; it should be followed by four further routes UNDER FRENCH MANAGEMENT running north–south: Stockholm–Vienna–Trieste; London–Paris–Dakar–Cape Town; Helsinki–Leningrad–Simferopol–Jerusalem; Oslo–Strasbourg–Benghazi. In addition, another four cross-routes linking east and west like latitude lines. This also assumed underground transportation networks beneath the future (at the time still ruined) metropolitan areas and an air traffic network; hover vehicles, airships, aviation platforms the size of football fields and a kind of flying hotel could be anticipated.

Brissot was looking forward to Europe; he thought of the bloodshed in two world wars as a kind of ideological fertilizer; nations, he said, which built such transport networks, did not go to war. Still full of the high spirits he had felt in Tübingen, he referred in Paris to the small engines of the Indian Imperial Railways as tailor-made in their sturdiness and elegance for the variations in altitude of northwestern India, and thus similarly suited to the mountain ranges of the Balkans. He referred to the bridges of the Yenisei. They were built by French engineers for the northern line of the Trans-Siberian Railway. Then the plan was changed in favour of a more southerly route. The bridges remained preserved in the middle of the Russian landscape, unused and undestroyed. The Musée Municipale de Paris, Brissot suggested, should build glass envelopes for these constructions on the spot and add them to their collection as a kind of open-air department, an outlying suburb of Paris, art of the Iron Age, a document of the European spirit 'lying around' in inhospitable Siberia, where, as the saying goes, not even grass grows. Without civilizing and exploiting Siberia, said Brissot, whose objections, demands and reports colleagues in the Foreign Ministry considered worth curbing, there would be no potent Europe. Every centre needs such colonies, in order to maintain the grammatical form of the subjunctive (the form of possibility) in its political language. Brissot said in 1947 that in order to protect the large biotope of Siberia, which was by that point destroyed by industrialization, one had to cover a few square kilometres of that country (preferably in the vicinity of the native iron culture) with a glass enclosure like a greenhouse; but not like a settlement on Mars: It's not the sphere of life that is being covered over with glass to develop like in a hothouse; rather, it's a museum sphere that guarantees calm and the absence of development in the face of civilization or the Europe machine that penetrates everything. Brissot says this will reach the Pacific in sixty years, that is, in 2007.

FIGURE 4. F. Brissot studying railway routes in the Balkans. The maps are from before the war. Which tunnels, which bridges have meanwhile been blown up? Europe realizes itself, says Brissot, as soon as it opens itself to the Orient. That was already the case when Bonaparte invaded Egypt.

FIGURE 5 (above). Old Europe. Thirteen seats in the saloon car of the Orient Express. In the background: a pianola. Mirrors inside the car supplement the passing landscape.

FIGURE 6 (below). European women at the so-called 'zero hour'. The new Europe.

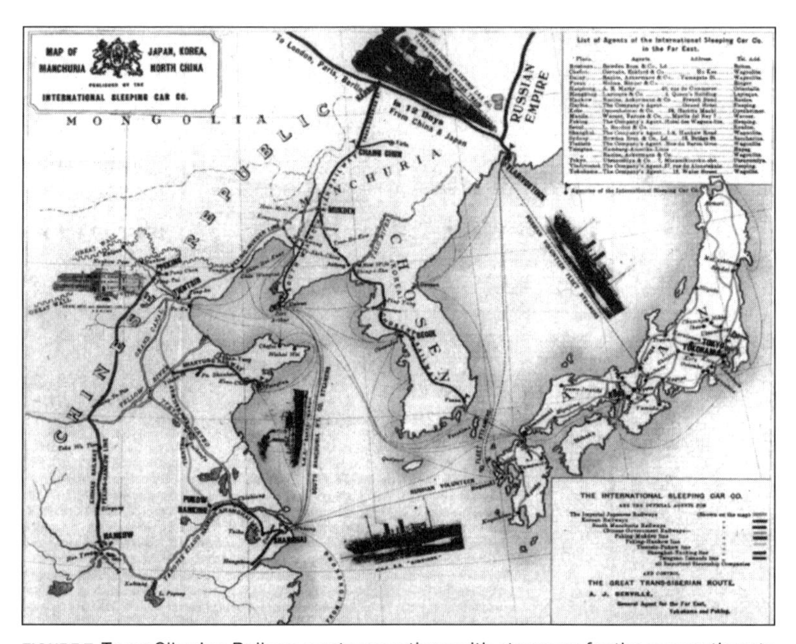

FIGURE 7. Trans-Siberian Railway, eastern sections with steamers for the connections to Japan. The railroad sets off the Japanese war against Russia, in which Russia loses Port Arthur. The INVESTMENTS IN IRON provoke Russia's defeat by Japan, the jealousy of the United States, and Japan's wars against China.

In Another Land

In the night, we crossed the border into Dagestan, i.e. we traversed mountains (the border is not marked anywhere). They searched for us with infrared sights on their helicopters. When we hear the machines in the distance, we lie down on the ground and place sheets of corrugated metal on top of our bodies. Thus our tell-tale body warmth is not detectable.

We had nothing with us except our weapons and the sheets of corrugated metal, which prevent the enemy from looking into our 'Islamic hearts'. Although the seat of courage for an Islamic Caucasian lies not in the heart or the solar plexus (where the Russian language places the seat of higher feelings), but rather in a gland, whose location I shall not write down, so that the enemy does not learn of it.

I was born in a small place on the West Bank, a settlement that could hardly be called a village. I grew up in camps. There's nothing superfluous about me, everything is circulation, determination and stored-up muscle, just what I need in order to move around. When everything has been confiscated from a person, they become a dangerous fighter. When we've conquered the country, into which we've been smuggled, we are vulnerable. That's why I like the initial movement of an undecided struggle best. Conversely, the victory, i.e. the administration of the conquered object, depresses me. These reflections passed through my mind as we drew the sheets of metal off our bodies and once again followed the path that leads us into the future. The noise of the rotors dissipated into the distance.

What Is Power of the 'Mind'?

The Dagestan authorities, Russian stooges, talked about borders. That's something we fighters of the faith cannot simply accept. Islam recognizes no borders such as were established by the colonialist Russians in the nineteenth century. Where in the mountains is there a border? That was rebel leader Kahteb's reply sent via the Internet to our correspondent who was in Tblisi.

Yes, where on the eastern slopes of the Caucasus, as it plunges down to the sea, should there be a border? I, Kahteb, born in and later expelled from West Jordan, ask: Where should the boundaries of my boundless faith lie? Or those of my fighters, whom I present to the international press? They would have to tear off our limbs bit by bit to get us out of the country. Then our anger turns against them and their helicopters fall to the ground, brought down by the power of the mind. Because they are aggressors against the land of faith, which extends from horizon to horizon.

The Conman and Happiness

Happiness takes the shape of passing hours. In the summer guesthouse. Here, he is safe. He can't always please the tall, quick-tempered woman, the heiress.

Often, she looks at his fox-like face sceptically. Then he turns to look at their two children eating noisily at the breakfast table. They are the time of his safety. Once these facts grow up, the mendacious beginning of his marriage will become overgrown like a thousand-year-old castle. And at some point, it will no longer make any difference how everything came together and grew together. Every day that passes and spares him, he gains a little bit of cover. In the end, he could confess everything by an open fire. Thus, he fills his belly at the breakfast table. He winks chummily at the tall person in jeans, who thinks of him as her husband. The peach tastes really good, he says, the conman.

Is One Allowed to Defend Oneself against a Helpless Man?

After twenty-four years of marriage to a cripple, Krimhild felt the question 'is one allowed' to be beside the point. A human being is allowed to do everything if she is in control of the circumstances and prevents her guilt from spreading.

There is, says Krimhild, really no practical application of the concept of guilt in private life, because the control which a person exercises alone behind closed doors makes that big word shrink. What shall I do, Krimhild asks her friend Frida. He can still move two fingers for a while, but only with the help of an appliance, which converts the movement into yes–no answers according to a digital pattern (01/02). That taps on my clitoris (or, if I instruct him, a bit to the side, say seven millimetres, that's not so bad, but as the years go by, that's the wrong place, too). That doesn't stoke one's pleasure or let one's imagination wander.

That's how, Krimhild says, I've managed this famous body for more than twenty years ('for seven years I bore it'). The soul of a child, a genius of the century, a good match, a contract entered into (ME, eighteen years old, before the onset of his illness). A wrapped present, which I only later learned to unwrap. Scholars have confirmed for me that I did not have to reckon with a cripple of this kind, 'through thick and thin by his side'.

I fed him, I treated him like a child. In the end, he only wanted his shoulders tickled, his bum stroked, and that always on a Saturday after he had finished his research or dictation. He dreaded idle Saturdays.

We came to an agreement that I should choose Guideon as a lover. But what's that: A prescribed, permitted lover? But nobody else? I was only allowed to use this reliable man to satisfy my physical needs. What does physical mean? What did the famous scientist know about 'use'? No human being can live like that permanently. A negative energy has accumulated, a resistance. I don't control it, it 'uses' me. *Nemo ultra posse obligatur*. I found it again as a quote in Arab translation in the course of my research in Toledo on Spanish texts of the high Middle Ages.

My cripple is not interested in texts.[19]

Solar Eclipse

He had set out from Koblenz at eight in the morning and wanted to get to Ulm. Nothing took him there except duty. The divorce judge was due to annul fifteen years of his life. That was Ulm. There was a sense of tidiness to it, no interest in anything new.

Behind the spectators of the BLACK SUN who had stopped on the autobahn to get out and look at the darkening rainy sky with black tape over their eyes, the police had closed the road in both directions. That's why he stood there on the highway with no interest in the celestial event, equally distant from his present life in Koblenz and the remains of his life in Ulm. The finally conclusive legal break could no longer be made that day.

---

19 *Nemo ultra posse obligatur*—an acknowledged legal principle of Roman lawyer Ulpian. No one is obliged to do more than he is capable of. The jurist Ulpian is concerned with FRONTIER RIVERS, as he calls them. There is an end to time, property has a boundary, there is a limit to the applicability of subjective value, there is a limit of intolerance applicable to actual people. Ulpian derives his legal principles from this.

The Consistency of the Moon

A valuable scrap of old material, whose transport back to Earth would have been more expensive than if it were sacrificed, had established CLARITY with its well-aimed impact near the lunar pole. The metal core of the Moon constituted, at most, 3 per cent of its volume. I assume, said Sigurd Wolfsson,[20] that a heavenly body the size of Mars collided with our Sun. The mass of the Moon escaped as a consequence. At first, it orbited very close to planet Earth. The Moon must have filled a third of the sky when it shone.

—For our ancestors?

—I don't think there were any ancestors yet.

—Perhaps single-celled organisms, who did not 'see' but, rather, felt?

—Every living thing feels something.

—And where did the Mars-sized planetary body disappear to?

—We'll find it far out in space. A misshapen piece of rubble that's still fairly big.

—Beyond Pluto?

—Well beyond that, a trans-Plutonian planet. A dark piece of rubble only visible against the light of the Sun. There, it's the size of a thumbnail. I don't think, therefore, that we'll get to see

---

20 Grandson of a Jewish lawyer, who emigrated from Breslau to Iceland in 1933. Established musical theory at the Reykjavik Music Academy. His sons became educational researchers or composers. The grandson is a space scientist. The Wolfsson dynasty are considered leaders in the investigation of outer space. This is curious, because the starry vault is least visible (due to fog and cloud) from Iceland. In fact, here, too, communication by words and signs is what counts. In South America, in the High Atlas and on Hawaii (or from earth's orbit) there is 'looking', in Iceland there is interpretation.

Earth's old companion, its collision partner, 'face to face' once again. Measure it, yes; see it, no.

—So no one saw this 'stroke of fate' then, which perhaps helped life to emerge on planet Earth?

—No one. But perhaps the TOTALITY OF THE EARTH was alive at that time. The earth as a giant living body, as it were. The giant Ymir, the old texts say, wounded and killed by a 'companion'.[21]

The Poets of Organization

The early Bolsheviks were city dwellers. They hated being sent out into the countryside to watch over the growth of decades (divided into Five-Year Plans) and the corn sprouting up. In the rooms of the Moscow headquarters, on the other hand, the props of the 'world' were on hand. The conspiracy of the class enemy, the organizational consolidation of one's own camp, those were swift processes. A quick mind was called for.

Whole regions are to be included in the budget in *one* fell swoop; it would take a single person years to rush through these landscapes by foot. As city dwellers, the young Bolsheviks resided in offices.

In 1921, a hardworking clique of such city dwellers, all unmasked as Trotskyists after 1924, were building up the ORGANIZATION TRUST. Apparently, an anti-Bolshevik resistance organization was being set up. It was said to have strong troops at its disposal; there were even participants in the conspiracy in high Party positions. This was how they challenged contact by Western secret services. The anarchist Savinkov, who was conspiring with Western powers, and the 'master spy' Sydney

21 The Russian scholar Hélène Blavatsky claims to have found texts in Tibetan monasteries confirming this information.

Reilly made contact with the organization. They were arrested and executed.

The plain-clothed townspeople were early risers. They translated the skills of a watchmaker and a counterfeiter into intelligence practices. After this operation in 1921, Great Russia was free of foreign agents and infiltrators for a short time. The political poets who organized TRUST could also have set up a party, if they had been instructed to do so. They owed the immense artificiality of their approach to the places they came from that all lay in the West still waiting for revolution.

Siberian Time Reserves

At the time when Comrade Andropov was head of the KGB and preparing himself for the position of Party general secretary—his health was always at risk and he was, therefore, immobile and averse to travel—one of the main sections of the Russian secret service had Kyrgyz Colonel Lermontov, whose ancestors included pagan priests (Siberian animists). During working hours, he compiled a collection of historical sketches. (In such a huge organization with worldwide operations, immense quantities of time slip away more slowly outside the windows of the towering concrete building than anywhere else in the world.) A number of these sketches dealt with 'paralysis at the decisive moment'.

It is an odd fact that the great evildoers of world history are often seized by paralysis and that at decisive moments. It would be doctrinaire to say, Lermontov insists, that there are no gods. It's evident that they make their appearance as either reinforcement or paralysis. Lermontov asked his listening comrades: Do you seriously want to hold a chill responsible for Napoleon's failure at Waterloo to fight the encirclement battle, which his generals advised and which would have guaranteed certain success? Do you want to explain the mistake by a chill?

No, replied one of the scholarly secret service assistants, because of the Emperor's disbelief in his own mission. The assistant was educating himself daily (in those days they were all educating themselves in preparation for Perestroika, the coming of which they had a premonition, without anyone knowing what name the new freedom would have).

I dispute that, responded Lermontov. The divinity paralysing him is the same one that struck a thunderbolt between the Trojans and the Greeks; Athena befuddled everyone's senses. She paralysed the Trojan's judgement, who shot his arrow at Menelaus; and she spoiled the flight of that arrow so that the Greek was only slightly wounded. The divine intervention was sufficient to destroy the brief peace between Trojans and Greeks. Only the gods can act with such precision and penetrate the day-to-day causal nexus of life by causing such devastation. If you chalk something like that up to a cold virus or a lack of sleep, then that seems doctrinaire to me.[22]

You say that as a materialist?

That's what I'm saying, replied Lermontov. A materialist is never doctrinaire. Without reason, he doesn't rule out *any* operation of worldly force as impossible. Especially not if it reveals itself to our observation. Take the strange blinding paralysis of Hitler (at the very moment of his failure on the front before Moscow). In December 1941: 'as if snow-blind'. He declares war on the United States. According to the treaties, he didn't have to

---

22 Lermontov is referring to the following incident: After the futile siege of Troy, the Greeks and Trojans have concluded an armistice. This happened on the advice of the majority of the gods. Helen is to be surrendered to her husband Menelaus. But then a lesser goddess, namely Athena, sabotages this peace agreement. Through divine pressure, she inspires a retainer of Paris (at the time, 'owner' of Helen) to kill Menelaus with an arrowshot. She moderates this divine influence (so that Menelaus is only wounded), because the pernicious arrow is sufficient even as a SIGN to destroy the armistice.

do it. He seals the end of the German Reich. How can you explain something like that if gods don't take a hand? Robespierre's paralysis at the moment of Thermidor is exactly the same. Likewise, Trotky's curious 'chill' during the crisis before Lenin's death. Why does he travel to the Caucasus at that decisive moment? It costs him his chance of power. I have here a collection of 12,000 striking examples. Do you want to ignore all of them?

I am very surprised, replied Lermontov's superior, who had joined the company. *What* exactly are you occupying yourself with, comrade?

The empire, which was still intact at the time, had all the time reserves of Siberia at its disposal. And consequently, the reserves thought as well. A safe deposit box for the inner life of the soul. In the bunkers of the KGB, the country's academic elites have lively interactions with the elites from the Academy of Sciences, who had established their seats in privileged centres by the rivers of Siberia.[23]

I (Gorbachev's last assistant) was reminded of Lermontov's collection as I observed the President's paralysis. It burst forth after his return from the conference in Madrid. We went there to beg. He was never again what he had been. A moody, Mediterranean god from antiquity, who helped destroy Troy at Athena's side, had forced his way into him (just like viruses, insect stings, poisons, serious disappointments do). So he sat in his room and did nothing, while the 'bush robbers of Minsk' hatched their plot

---

23 Akademgorodok near Novosibirsk has 60,000 posts. The generously subsidized city of science is globally linked to the networks of international research; in Akademgorodok itself there are no outside distractions. In winter, a three-yard-high hill is just about enough for sledging. A hike to the north, east, west or south would have no goal that could be named. In autumn, walls of fog, in winter, snow immobilizes everything. In summer, the absence of coolness; there is no transition between the seasons. Like the sparseness of a medieval monastery, thinkers are surrounded by a pure reserve of living time.

and expropriated the commonwealth. Should he have arrested them for high treason? He had the authority.

We buried Lermontov shortly after the accident at Chernobyl. 'Abandoned by all the gods', he had shot himself.

The Glowing Block in the Balance; the Diver Ananenko

A telephone connection between Moscow and the *Frankfurter Rundschau* newspaper

—Are you ready to record everything, Frankfurt?

—I'm ready.

—Then I'll start.

—Can you hear me all right?

—I can hear you.

—I'll now read the text.

—You can start.

—The calamity comes from a plant that the periodical *Literaturna Ukraina* described in harsh terms: disorganization, bunglers . . .

—What kind of article?

—Title, colon, quote, *Not a private matter*, unquote. Author: Liubov Kovalevska.

—Can you please spell that.

—L-i-u-b-o-v, new word, K-o-v-a-l-e-v-s-k-a. I'm quoting word-for-word, colon, quote, The disorganization has not only undermined discipline, but also the sense of responsibility for the shared outcome of the work . . . A general weariness and deterioration became apparent . . . unquote.

—When was that?

—The article was published one month before the accident.

—A month *before* the accident?

—Right.

—Please continue.

—On 25 April, at 8 a.m., warning devices show one of the fuel rods overheating. The power station is shut down immediately. The heat, however, continues to spread. No one can go to or look at the rod itself. It's assumed that hydrogen has formed through contact between steam and metal (just like Zeppelins that exploded). This gas explodes. That was seventeen and a half hours after the first damage.

—Seventeen and a half hours?

—Yes. On 26 April, at 1.30 a.m. The explosion catapulted the roof and the reactor cover into the night sky. Only then did all emergency and cooling systems fail. The naked eye finally sees something. Graphite blocks, in which the fuel elements are embedded, begin to burn. The reactor core melts (this cannot be seen). Above ground, flames and steam rise up into the night sky.

—Flames and steam.

—An engineer gets locked in the control room; he can no longer be reached from the entrances to the plant. He keeps himself busy by monitoring the event. He can be reached by telephone. Later, aircraft drop 5,000 tons of lead, cement and flame-retardant chemicals on the reactor.

—What kind of chemicals?

—That couldn't be ascertained. It says flame-retardant chemicals. The drop is stopped by an intervention from E. Velikhov.

—Spell, please.

—E-v-g-e-n-y, new word, V-e-l-i-k-h-o-v.

—The adviser to the general secretary?

—The very same one. It's feared that the weight of 5,000 tons of sand, lead and other material, which is 'intended to bury the reactor', will push the reactor core down. Quote. The core of reactor block 4 is incandescent. It constitutes a hot, radioactive zone, which is somehow held in balance. Unquote.

—No one knows how something like that is maintained?

—That's the problem. An attempt is made to drive a tunnel under the power station, in order to block the reactor from there with a mass of lead, concrete and boron.

—Was that it?

—There is still some more . . .

—We've got another four minutes.

—Below the reactor there are two basins. They're separated from one another and the reactor by concrete walls; they are intended to absorb steam. There was still water in these basins. The reactor core has already broken through to the first basin.

—First basin as in the upper basin?

—The basins sit side by side.

—But broken through in the meantime?

—Immediately after the explosion. Another new explosion happens immediately thereafter.

—Go on . . .

—The water chamber must be emptied; the mechanic Alexei Ananenko dives down with two colleagues.

—Spell that, please.

—A-n-a-n-e-n-k-o.

—Can he be described as a diver? Diver Ananenko?

—He's really a mechanic. He could have refused. But he is the only man on the shift who knows where the shutoffs are that must be turned underwater.

—So that it drains away . . .

—Exactly. He found them . . . is immediately flown to the capital for treatment. I leave out the references to the various collective decisions and how they were arrived at, there would be too many names.

—That's all right.

—Have you got everything?

—Everything.

—All the best.

—All right. Bye!

There was still one minute and twenty seconds of transmission time left. The doors to the transmission room only opened after this period expired. The reporter, who had sent greetings to his homeland, had *time to reflect*.

A Near Disaster

Speaking very generally: Men and gods do not meet one another directly. They occupy counter-worlds that respond to one another. To that extent, they are dependent on one another. Whether they also believe that is beside the point.

Thus spoke the ataman of Novosibirsk.[24] He based himself on the episcopate of Alexandria, was later taken to the Bosphorus, evacuated from there to Kyiv and is now deposited in Siberia. In antiquity, catastrophe was only a hairbreadth away. When parallel worlds touch, they obliterate one another.

The berserker Diomedes stormed into battle before the walls of Troy. His chariot groaned under his weight, as the goddess Athena swung herself up beside her protégé. In her impassioned exuberance ('Head of passion' = Athena), she felt the eyes of

---

24 Little appreciated by the scientists in Akademgorodok.

Diomedes while the steeds rushed forward, guided by their own eyes; she opened the berserker's gaze to the gods (and thus to possibilities) otherwise inaccessible to the human gaze as such (whoever sees possibilities will immediately perish, but an encryption prevents this gaze until death). The furious Diomedes sees Aphrodite, a friend of the Trojans. He wounds the sparkling-eyed goddess on her thigh. Ares, the god of war, likewise a Trojan friend, approaches. Diomedes wounds the god with his lance. Athena, crouching on the shaft of the chariot, whips the crazy hero forward. Is this a civil war between the gods? Is it like positive and negative matter about to annihilate one another?

The council of gods consults faster than light. Its will is indeed the only factor that functions faster than light. They decide: Diomedes must atone for having 'seen' the gods. And for 'attacking' a god. The gods comforted the wounded Aphrodite, the seriously injured Ares (without whom there would be no 'war', no 'fostering of violence'; rather, only the completely 'unrestrained' eruption of the destructive principle would be real, which stops at the gods as little as the antibodies in which we live). Thus, the heretical Diomedes—heretical was, however, only Athena's influence on him—was destroyed by a few bolts of lightning. Not even ashes remained of him. It was as if the berserker had never existed. His parents and ancestors, sorted into demigods and rebels, crumbled into nothing. The scheming goddess Athena, energetic and factional, went unpunished. No one learned that she had almost caused a disaster: the simultaneous devastation and destruction of the world of men *and* the world of the gods.

A New Age

All men are equal (after the revolution). But the sense of time, in which a person moves, is not. Comrade Bogdanski only had to look at the water faucets, the technical inlay, in a hotel in Lemberg (Lviv) to go numb with longing. These taps were installed by plumbers or suppliers trained in Vienna. Bogdanski wanted to rush to the nearest state library, to a cheap hotel, where a liaison lasts an afternoon and not seventeen years. This sense of time is the receptacle of life and works like a drug.

Bogdanski was far enough away from Lemberg. He was responsible for the re-education of delinquent youths, members of captured gangs. The Party is working on altering the sense of time. The re-education of individual lads from youth gangs proceeds more slowly than corn grows.

The acceleration of one million years was included in a training analysis by a sage from Vienna. Historical periods multiply one another when they touch. That's how the soul works. The articles in the *ROTE FAHNE* and in the commentaries from the *Leipziger Volkszeitung* encompassed the whole passage of time since Spartacus. What a flying creature! What a dragon!

In a cafe in the middle of Berlin, comrades are talking heatedly about the uprising in central Germany. This uprising was prepared during the early industrial revolution. What does that mean? It was prepared much earlier during the Peasants' Wars. As we talk, the decisive moment of the uprising draws closer. Minutes of revolutionary conspiracy corresponded to ten years of life before. Greedy, says one, the new age is greedy.

'Criminal youths' are lying in a barn about two hundred yards from the cottage where Bogdanski is writing his notes. In the absence of a telegraph, writing notes links him with every horizon. He must improve his Russian; beyond that he really should be able to speak more confidently in dialect. His Red Army men guard the camp of the young, disarmed bandits. They reply when he addresses them in his untaught Russian. With his own squad, the situation remains akin to an interrogation.

He has the impression that the 'juvenile criminals' don't change at all. There's no learning or re-education. They learn to play-act, i.e. they express their will when they want something. On the other hand, he senses a change in himself: His desire to get away from here grows enormous. He'd like to have a task that can be realized quickly and that's in line with the standards of western cities. The theory that collective work improves the young delinquents is fading. They can, it is said, be turned into Soviet people (it can take seven to twelve years), perhaps into an especially vital type, since their criminal energy (some are murderers) represents in a materialist sense a supplementary force, which expresses itself through performance when transformed. If only there weren't the uncanny LENGTH OF TIME for the transformation.

The Immortal Woman

A 500,000-German-Mark Investment
for a Body 1 Gram in Weight

The black fabric that covers her body, which is only for leaving the beach, cost 20,000 DM. She carries golden shoes with rhinestones in her hand as she walks across cheap sand. An enormous bag of pale crimson leather, whose colour a layman could take to be pink, is slung over her shoulder.[25] She has lost weight. For every one gram of body weight, an annual investment of 500,000 DM is made. If the investment were doubled and if, from an economic point of view, such an output affected 400,000 such valuable subjects, an industrial breakthrough could be achieved.

25 The colour crimson is produced from 20,000 snails, as far as the concrete bag of pale crimson leather is concerned.

First: to 'eternal youth'; but since nothing in this world remains constant and only defensively so: to immortality.

A Memorial to Unknown Soldiers

After the October Revolution, the administrative districts of the Crimea remained 'unsupervised' by headquarters for a while. The local regimes were neither 'red' nor 'white', but rather 'provincial'. One such local drumhead court martial executed a number of officers, of whom it is not known whether they were obeying the Soviet leadership *or* one of the many counter-revolutionary hierarchies. A visitor from Kerch ordered that the shot men be sent to the bottom of the sea a few hundred yards from the coast with lead weights on their feet. Later, divers found the dead; they were standing upright on the seabed, swaying back and forth in a row 'as if for all eternity'. The divers' reports were confused. They refused to bring up the dead. In the meantime, the Crimea was occupied by General Wrangel's 'white troops'. After that, Wrangel was driven out again. In 1945, when divers[26] were once again searching for mines or hidden midget submarines in front of the palace of Prince Felix Yussopov, the row of dead was still swaying, somewhat ragged, but in rows on the seabed, invisible from the shore.

—Was it not a tad extravagant to attach valuable lead to their feet? To throw valuable lead away after throwing away the already valueless dead? In times of revolutionary shortages?

---

26 The purpose this time was the preparation of the (Yalta) conference of the Allies, for which a British delegation led by Prime Minister Churchill and a US delegation led by President Roosevelt was awaited. It was thought possible that submarines of the Axis powers could deposit explosive devices on the beaches or in shallow water.

—The lumps of lead must have been readily available from some delivery or maybe they were stranded in Crimea. Lead plus the hooks for the retaining cables that attached the former to the feet of the dead. That couldn't have been quickly produced in the Crimea and still less so in the Prince's palace. It was valuable, but not valuable here, where it was at most a lost object of value, for which there was no other use. The lead was no doubt no more needed than the dead.

—But there seems to me to be an intensity to the action, a particular need of expression behind this course of action in 1918. They could have been buried. No, they found lead weights and materialized their idea of attaching them to the feet of the dead. They must have had a picture in their minds like the one the divers later saw, a row of shot men swaying back and forth at the bottom of the sea. Perhaps they had doubts whether it was right to shoot these people and they expressed these doubts. It reminds me of sausages swinging in a chimney.

—But who is 'they'? We know nothing about the 'visitor from Kerch' or the members of the court martial. It was an anonymous local event.

—Which put up its own memorial and which demonstrably lasted until 1945. They were armed?

—Of course, otherwise they wouldn't have been able to shoot the officers. But who are 'they'? And who are the officers? If it were not for the divers' reports, I would say: it's propaganda, a rumour spread by White Guards . . .

—Or Bolshevik atrocity propaganda turned around by White Guards. Is there anything to say that these weren't Reds killed by Whites?

—The dead were in uniform. It should be possible to draw conclusions from that.

—Did the Reds walk around naked? Did they not have any uniforms?

—There remains a curious need for expression. They must have had something in mind when they dropped the corpses into the sea, and that with weights that were hanging from the feet of the dead. They went to a lot of bother.

—Yes, they got hold of boats or small ships. Also, a device to heave the dead overboard.

—Yes, because there's no other way of getting out to the spot where the dead are swaying in the water, where they, like hanged men, swayed as if in the wind. That's an image for you.

—But one that no one sees. Except for the diver who's been instructed to take a look down there. They wanted to show something and at the same time hide something.

—It's certainly curious.

—Very curious indeed. But that's the wrong word. You can't imagine, my friend, how terrible it is for a diver to see these ghosts swaying back and forth amidst the seaweed of the Black Sea with the gentle movements that the tides impose at this depth.

—Propelled yard by yard closer to Turkey over the years. What else did the divers say?

—They had been horrified. As if they'd seen ghosts.

—For a moment, they thought the dead were ghosts?

—As something intended for them. They saw a message in it for themselves.

—A curious result of the Revolution.

—Or the counter-revolution. That's exactly what's not known, what it was *locally*.

—Then we can say: a curious funeral.

—Yes. But don't keep on saying 'curious'. The word isn't appropriate at all.

—Don't be petty.

—This way of propping the dead up at the bottom of the sea, it seems mysterious to me.

—You can say that again.

—A mystery that expresses something.

—Yes, because it's underwater.

—You must imagine it in the light of the divers' lamps. There were seven dead in a row. But the spaces between them varied.

—Could the divers identify anyone?

—Only that they were human beings and not phantoms.

—But they thought they were ghosts?

—Yes, in a manner of speaking. They had no suitable word for what they saw. As the saying goes, 'half mad with fear'. There is no half madness.

—Why not? Half gripped by madness, half down-to-earth?

—That's impossible.

—But one is never quite normal, and madmen, as you know, are never completely mad.

—No, here, I think, one must make a clear decision: either mad or not. Just as one can't be 'half pregnant'.

—That's taking us away from the subject, and we don't have to decide that.

—Above all, because the reports of the divers, at least those from 1918, remain unclear.

—The whole business is unclear.

—But it's expressive.

—That's what I'm telling you!

A Visit to Robert Musil in 1942

On a March day in 1942, Daniel Wilde, a naturalized US citizen, had a taxi take him from Zurich to a suburb of Geneva. As an art collector he had information that a 'valuable' writer or scholar lived there; it seemed a good prospect to acquire original works cheaply from the impoverished artist. Wilde, a businessman born near Oschersleben and forced to become an emigre, had a fine REVERENCE FOR ART. He was interested in strange people who produced ART, and apart from that he searched for profitable opportunities. The artistic mind, the exchange of sources of intelligence, is communicative: from these communications emerge rare unique specimens, things of value, which buyers at auctions go wild for. Thus, Wilde travelled the coasts of the continent, insofar as they were not yet occupied (southern France, Portugal, Spain and then, with the aid of an airline, Switzerland and Sweden) in search of treasures and routes by which emigres were forced to offer up such treasures for sale. For acquisitions he had assured himself of clients. The spring of 1942 was unique, a great chance. In this respect, the very industrious Wilde was in a hurry. The drive from Zurich to Geneva began to bore him. He had nevertheless made up his mind to give some time to the strange man whose work had hardly any contemporary readers, even though the title of one of his books had spread around the world like a catchphrase.

Wilde was superficial. It was the only way the businessman could avoid becoming entangled and still get an overview. He saw very quickly that there was nothing to buy here. The stubborn man, plagued by the effects of a stroke (this was not something Wilde had observed, but had heard about), was mainly occupied with making fair copies of chapters of a long novel that was not yet completed. The work dealt with a period of perhaps twelve to twenty years, all of whose themes date back to before the First World War. At this time, as Wilde knew it, there were hardly any readers on the US market for this time period. He listened patiently to what the famous, wretched (in a spiritual sense: 'emaciated') man told him. How can anyone capriciously describe the dim past when so many interesting and dangerous things are happening on the continent?

Wilde had his taxi called. He wanted to get to the Engadine that same day where there were paintings to buy. He would have liked to help the ailing old man. But there was nothing to be found in this house for which he could have made an offer, apart from the house itself. Furthermore, Wilde had the impression that the stubborn man didn't want to sell anything. He wanted to be successful, but not to sell anything. The whole day could be said to be sunny.

A Story of a Tyrant

> 'The question why the great historian
> Did not write the long-awaited
> Fourth volume of his *HISTORY OF ROME*
> The one about the Empire
> Still preoccupies historians today in the . . . '
>
> Heiner Müller, *Mommsens Block*

The sole spokesman of Tiberius and commander of the Praetorian Guard was a man named Sejanus. Because at a certain point in time no one could trust him any more, he had to be tricked and arrested by the Emperor himself and killed in his presence. In those decades, power accrued for the ruler and the few people he trusted like a parasitical plant. It was ascribed to the Emperor and he could refuse it, as he wished. Whatever he had never said or ordered grew around him into decisions, which were attributed to him from a distance. If future thoughts of the ruler were drawn into the calculation, then there was no longer anything to which speculation could not have been directed.

Recently, however, a similar centre of gravity had formed around the SPOKESMAN OF THE EMPEROR, the observer of everything and the master of everyday access to Tiberius.

Sejanus, the Emperor's spokesman, prefect of the Praetorians, saw that the Emperor feared him, and thus he feared the Emperor. The possible exercise of power, no matter whether that of the Emperor or of the mighty Sejanus, is anticipated by their clientele, the countless dependants, foes and friends who all have more time than those in power. Such 'attributed power' cannot be held onto like houses, slaves or money. Until then, the Prefect Sejanus, battle-tried, resolute and Tiberius's close friend for many years, had taken no measures to overthrow Caesar. He did, however, have the means at his disposal to do so; he commanded guard contingents who had not seen Caesar personally. It would be possible to present these men a different person other than Caesar and then have Caesar arrested as an assassin and killed. There is no indication that Sejanus intended such a thing. It was enough that he could not avoid knowing, that Caesar could assume that he could do such a thing.

This was the direction in which Tiberius' reflections were moving. He tended to think slowly and then act swiftly before his thoughts became muddled again. Thus he had Sejanus arrested and quickly killed. His fortune was seized and his clientele sent into exile.

Sejanus' Two Children

The Emperor had come to no decision regarding the two children, the lad still a minor and the daughter not yet old enough to marry, i.e. she was not yet eleven years of age. When asked the question what was to be done with them, he turned away. They were thus condemned.

The executioner, however, was forbidden by the law—it wintered over in the midst of this despotism and threatened those who contravened it without direct, precise orders from the sovereign—to kill young women if they had not yet met a man. Thus, he 'first had to be intimate with this child before he beheaded her'. At this point, the son of Sejanus was already lying in the sand, which absorbed his blood.

This narrative by Tacitus doesn't correspond to the truth, however. It serves to educate posterity, which is to be reminded of the category of a righteous life by shocking stories of tyrants. In fact, the executioner exchanged the daughter of Sejanus for a Syrian slave girl, whom he killed on the sand; on the other hand, he took the daughter of Sejanus into his house; her granddaughter became a Christian, a distant relative was still alive in the time of Emperor Constantine. For his act of deception, the executioner avoided a serious impropriety.

'Shore of Fate'

It was two years before the fall of the Wall. Our discussion concerned the children of Sejanus. Heiner Müller, who related the tragic incident according to his notes and the text by Tacitus, did not feel competent to provide a commentary. We were not yet used to talking to one another. It was our first scheduled dialogue, an attempt at suspicion. He was surprised at having to speak from the start on camera and was also not prepared to provide details. He asked that Tacitus be the subject of the conversation.

ME. What grips you most about the text?

MÜLLER. The Emperor.

ME. In what way?

MÜLLER. He has no influence on the execution of the children. Nor on the fact that the little girl is saved. He makes no contribution to the action at all. Everything is ascribed to him.

He draws a train of responsibilities behind him. That's power. It consists not of DOING, but of attribution.

ME. Does that still exist today?

MÜLLER. In the case of Stalin, yes.

ME. What about in the age of the gods, the emperors or even in the age of Bismarck?

MÜLLER. During the Roman empire.

ME. Would you write such a story as a text?

MÜLLER. No.

ME. Why not?

MÜLLER. It is a text.

ME. What about continuing it? What about taking a text and extending it into a play?

MÜLLER. It's already been extended. Having just come to the throne, Frederick II of Prussia cannot immediately prevent the burning of a witch. His ministers say: The sentence is final. The king's decree may be valid for all subsequent judgements; he cannot, however, rescind existing ones. If the law is not applied, a world will be lost. The king did not believe that. He had the condemned woman spirited away behind a scenery of smoke and fire and brought to safety in a barracks. Then he married off the witch with one of his hussars.

ME. Who helped him sabotage the execution?

MÜLLER. He had the square cordoned off by a battalion of soldiers. Cavalrymen brought the young woman to safety.

ME. Did the spectators see that?

MÜLLER. No. I'm not even certain that the judicial officers saw through what happened. Lots of fire in the foreground. The military (pioneers) had taken over the lighting of the pyre, no one was disappointed. The spectacle was not cancelled.

ME. And he arranged a marriage with one of those soldiers?

MÜLLER. One of the cavalries. He's said to have been a homosexual officer. His existence was now bound to the saved woman for life. The king had a sadistic inclination. He was an operator. He had a sharp mind.

ME. But he wasn't credited with the good deed because no one knew about it?

MÜLLER. No. That is the difference between the power of the Emperor or Stalin and the delicate position of a Prussian king.

ME. Assuming that a senior official listens to you. Would you tell him tales of Prussian virtue as Kleist once did?

MÜLLER. No one listens to me.

ME. What grips you about a text from classical antiquity when you're writing?

MÜLLER. I'm not gripped by anything. I just write.

ME. As an expression of life?

MÜLLER. Yes. This expression alongside other expressions of life.

ME. Tacitus wants to educate. You don't?

MÜLLER. (*doesn't reply*)

ME. What is useful about texts that are 2,000 years old?

MÜLLER. (*doesn't reply*)

ME. Is it legal formalism? The girl has to be deflowered first, so that she can be executed.

MÜLLER. The attribution of power to Stalin is THE IMPERIUM. A cloud of assumptions, suspicions, actual deeds, sham trials, executions. In this atmosphere, people change their characteristics, they display 'undreamt-of powers'. There is the REVOLUTIONARY RECONSTRUCTION OF MAN. It takes place in the BIOSPHERE OF THE IMAGINATION. Thus, the extraordinary power of Rome, this bloodthirsty, pitiless power machine becomes posthumously a METAPHOR. People would not take it up if they did not have a desire to do so. That's where Stalin's power lies. We are too superstitious to wish directly for happiness, and need the Medusa head of a grotesquely borne unhappiness that locks up the place of utopia and preserves its. The entrance must not be betrayed.

ME. Is that what the gods say . . . ?

MÜLLER. Both Emperor and Stalin fulfil this function.

ME. You don't consider Stalin himself to be grotesque?

MÜLLER. He's not even really bloodthirsty.

ME. Primitive?

MÜLLER. Not intellectual. Revolutionaries are all intellectuals, i.e. they don't need any 'haze of power'. They break down the whole world into details, of which no one is afraid. That's careless, says Stalin. Because then anyone (even a cook, which doesn't denote a rank but a non-analytical trained worker, a 'mixer') can solve problems, then we could live directly and take for ourselves whatever makes us happy. In 1937, all of them died because of this foolishness.

ME. No intellectual revolutionaries survived?

MÜLLER. No. The director of the Party's archive. A few. They're atheists, republicans like Brutus, opponents of the Emperor. You can't build empires with people like that.[27]

ME. Must one build empires?

MÜLLER. No. But if one wants to change human beings, then one has to.

ME. Real change, or only apparent change?

---

27 Bukharin is supposed to have lived on until 1944. He was not shot after being sentenced, says Müller, but kept on as an adviser. Stalin then discovered that he didn't need Bukharin's advice. There was no need to *dissect* the political. In actuality, the revolutionaries were unable to achieve anything practical. They could write articles, found organizations. Even their laws and plans are newspaper articles.

MÜLLER. Apparent change is enough. People behave for a long time as if they were changed.

ME. And then fall back to earth again?

MÜLLER. When 'power' comes to an end. When the gods withdraw their breath from Troy, Troy falls, no matter whether by cunning or force.

ME. Is the nineteenth century materialist?

MÜLLER. The doctrine of materialism killed the nineteenth century. The objective gaze is also unrealistic, because everything moves, and it doesn't move for objective reasons.

ME. Not even volcanoes or sand?

MÜLLER. In the power bloc, natural laws don't apply. Even in nature they don't apply absolutely. The gods inhabit the GAPS in the laws.

ME. Tacitus already no longer believes in the gods.

MÜLLER. But he appeals to them constantly. He doesn't list the dead killed by the emperors, because the audience at the Roman circus or the senators, who manage their estates, might rise up against the Emperor, but because the gods (who live not because we believe in them) dispose of a penal authority. The 'shore of fate'. Where the waters surge forward and the dams don't hold. Materialism is the building of dams.

ME. Lenin would write that you were under the 'suspicion of idealism'.

MÜLLER. Ideas are not the antithesis of materialism. The antithesis is violation. Nature violates its own rules. The nineteenth century knows of no *underground*. Those who are socially at the bottom don't orientate themselves according to this position, but rather to the lights shining above.

ME. Back to the Emperor. Do you think the little girl was saved?

MÜLLER. The executioner would have been unable to say anything about it. Not under the subsequent emperors either. He would have had to remain silent for more than sixty years. Tacitus would have been unable to find out about it, if it did happen.

ME. He says, the girl was executed.

MÜLLER. How?

ME. Thrown into the chasm from the Tarpeian Rock and strangled beforehand.

MÜLLER. Why that?

ME. An irreproachable execution is required. The gods are offended if the child takes hours to die at the foot of the rock with twisted limbs, or if she desperately defends herself. The dead of Albuquerque are knocked out with an injection, if not already killed, and only then exposed to two minutes of current in the electric chair.

MÜLLER. Why are you so certain that Sejanus' daughter could not be saved?

ME. Where in the system should the 'good will' come from that saves her? If it were there, the whole 'atmosphere' of imperial power would escape through this gap. A system of rules is watertight.

Reader-Friendly Articles Must Tell Their Stories Spatially

In January 1991, a few highly qualified palaeontologists waited in line following the dissolution of the GRD; they specialized in such early historical periods that only eight to twelve experts in their field existed in the world.

As a result, these scholarly specimens couldn't quickly move from the queue into new posts. Palaeontologists throughout the world were fighting for their survival. What remained was popularization, the commercial exploitation of a scholarship that deals with real conditions but sounds like belief in miracles.

The female correspondent of a Russian newspaper, wrestling with the transition to the new public spheres of St Petersburg and Moscow, was prepared to interview one of the experts. With a view of the Palace of the Republic from a window niche in the Palast Hotel, both tried to court the interest of paying readers.

AUTHORITY. I'm talking about the Cambrian explosion.

JOURNALIST. Explosion is good. That will interest readers.

AUTHORITY. After that, 96 per cent of all species are lost. Suddenly.

JOURNALIST. In a single catastrophic night?

AUTHORITY. Let's say in fifty million years or a bit more . . .

JOURNALIST. That's not fast.

AUTHORITY. Not in our terms. All further development emerges from 4 per cent of living matter. If the figures (that is, the breadth of the destruction) were displaced a little, and only 2.5 per cent of the living matter had been left over, then we would have died along with the rest.

JOURNALIST. That's a little abstract for the Russian reader, isn't it?

AUTHORITY. Why?

JOURNALIST. Should they imagine dinosaurs struck dead by a comet?

AUTHORITY. There aren't any dinosaurs yet!

JOURNALIST. What then? 96 per cent of species diversity is destroyed. One would first of all have to describe how 'species diversity' is to be imagined back then. What would you have there?

AUTHORITY. Voracious creatures. Four completely different designs in the construction plan as to what an animal should become. Four completely different structural blueprints as to what a creature should be.

JOURNALIST. How big?

AUTHORITY. Perhaps 12 mm. Dreadful monsters. They incessantly must devour other animals. They're devouring machines.

JOURNALIST. They would have to be shown as enlarged images!

AUTHORITY. You could do that. In the Cambrian explosion there emerges a diversity we are unable to grasp. This diversity is destroyed again, and out of the remaining life there emerge new diversities, e.g. joints and bones. After that, nothing fundamentally new happens for a long time. Until now. Because recently we have begun to develop entirely mental skeletons, without which we could no longer live. Today, new living organisms are emerging from an earthly remnant.

A few weeks later, the authority was unexpectedly discovered and appointed to a chair at Sydney University. This news and not his rare scholarship became the content of the article, which the Russian journalist sold in Moscow: the rescue of a scholar from socialism's elite circles by a city university in the Antipodes.

A Sudden Outbreak of Defeatism

'If the heart is emptied
if the heart is emptied
it will never be filled again . . . .'

French popular song of 1804

The chasseurs created a windbreak with blankets that they attached to poles (borrowed from the artillery). On the near side of this cover, they scraped away the snow down to the bare earth. This produced a hollow, into which one could descend by steps made of snow. In this hollow, on saddles and blankets, lay the much-loved commander, whose recovery none of those standing around believed in much longer. The chasseurs remained there standing, not because it was of any use, but because the spot was sheltered from the wind.

It was a depressing night followed by the brief light of the day of battle.[28] In another place and at another time, a valuable cavalry commander like Baron D'Houtpol would have been saved by amputation. In the late afternoon, a cannon ball shattered his thigh. Mixed up in the wound of the doomed man was a sticky pulp of bones, clothing, flesh and shell splinters. The division's doctors didn't venture to operate on such a wound in the night-time cold.

In the days after D'Houtpol's death, cavalrymen, officers, doctors reproached themselves. What had cast a spell on them during that cold night that they had not managed to do anything tangible to save their idol except erect a windbreak, i.e. a kind of provisional grave? They should have, that much was certain in retrospect, sent for one of the great surgeons on the staff of

---

28 At Preussisch-Eylau the sun only penetrated the scene of the battle for about half an hour. The remaining time: belated dawn light, premature dusk, snowstorm, thick clouds, which the soldiers confused with twilight.

the Guard; the art of radical amputation was an achievement in the last six months; they should have lit a fire instead of excavating a cold hollow. The direct contact with the bare earth, which conserved the cold better than the snow, was harmful. Later, Army Surgeon Baron Larrey said, General D'Houtpol, a god on horseback, could have been saved 'with a probability bordering on certainty and for many years served as an officer, who, transported in a container between two horses, could have commanded an attack even after the loss of a leg.'

Do you see, Murat, said the Emperor at about 3 p.m. on the day of the battle, do you see the columns over there, advancing over the hill to the right of the church. They want to crush (*écraser*) us. Do we wish to let them? With that, the vigorous Murat threw the whole cavalry of the French army at this point in the battle. Meanwhile, the scene was once again rendered invisible by a snowstorm. The Emperor had only seen the Russian army's advancing main force for a moment. A glance at the map suggested it must have been around the vicinity of the Preussisch-Eylau cemetery hill. The Russians' thrust was aimed at the centre of the French deployment.

Nothing from the French lines could be directed on foot to this location in time. Only the cavalry divisions were swift enough to disrupt the enemy's columns. Five times they broke through the enemy columns, which were swarming out into lines but were too slow to adjust their defences to the cavalry masses breaking through them.[29]

---

29 The masses of cavalry were, in turn, not suitable for forming a defensive line. To that extent, fighting here—thrown against one another because of a lack of time—were weapons systems that could not respond to one another. They could disrupt one another but not decide anything.

Seven times D'Houtpol rode through the Russian front at the head of the chasseurs, 'as one tears paper'.[30] Arriving at the rear of the attackers, this 'god of speed' had his men turn around and broke through backwards to the French lines. There, he drew up the squadrons once more in order again to attack, unnerve and break up the forcefully advancing column. Dusk fell, the armies bivouacked in the wind and snow. At this point, no one knew that next morning the Russian army opposite them would have marched off to the northeast.

Years later, during the RUSSIAN CAMPAIGN, an adjutant of D'Houtpol, Colonel St Martin, remembered the death-night at Preussisch-Eylau. The memory came back because it was asserted that D'Houtpol would have saved the mass of the cavalry even under the conditions of the retreat and the Russian winter. In a swift passage through to Minsk and without making any allowances for the slower artillery and infantry, the optimist, aware of the sluggish tendency of Russian consciousness, would have brought the cavalry back and immediately, after recharging his senses (by going from a meaningless location to a more meaningful one), put it on parade again and saved the army with fresh courage.

—What would he have wanted to do in Minsk?

—To tank up on confidence.

—How does one do that?

---

30 A report in the periodical *Moniteur*. The metaphor, however, is not precise. On the spot it means a dangerous melee, in which the slow-moving Russian grenadiers made way, as best they could, for the horses. Behind the riders, the column closed up again so nothing was 'torn', except insofar as concrete men were harmed by projectiles or blades.

—By connecting with a street map linked to Europe's network of roads. Confidence follows from the idea that, if necessary, one *could* reach Italy or Paris by a decent road. Once this idea is established, the cavalry troops can once more advance into the desert of snow. It's a matter of having ORIENTATION.

—Outwardly, it's the same cavalrymen, the same cold, the same wasteland.

—Yes, they shiver as before and are already as hungry as before. But they have changed the direction of attack from something that didn't make sense to something that did.

—But now D'Houtpol is dead.

That's what occurred to the adjutant. What he didn't know: It might have been possible to activate the will of the doomed commander on the night of Preussisch-Eylau if they 'had warmed his heart'. Perhaps during the many hours of waiting the fading man would have roused himself to give the order that they should at last call the head surgeon of the army to his side. The cavalrymen would have obeyed. There are hidden reserves in the doomed man (ideas, the body's resistance).

An idol at the balls of Paris as well, D'Houtpol had numerous lovers. Had they been with him that night, they could not have helped him. They would not have recognized him in his shattered state. His nurse, on the other hand, a Breton, would have been able to help; by reciting verses, she could have at least supplied the energy, which in a defeatist moment would have been sufficient to fetch a specialist.

'Then that rotten ship, my heart
Will rest at anchor in the harbour
The stirring infant pain
Find sleep in my breast.'

In the night of Preussisch-Eylau, those who stood around the general laid out in the hollow (and who felt a little warmer than it was outside) had no notion what they should do with this immortal commander. Death dragged on. A number of officers deliberated whether (for lack of any other anaesthetic) they should cut the throat of their suffering superior officer; or should he be stunned by a blow from a heavy sabre? The rasping would be replaced by silence.

But they were also afraid of this silence. They had misgivings about inflicting pain on their superior, which was something not provided for in the rules of war. Always ready for change, they easily inspired, behaved conventionally, and at the same time despised themselves because they had no tools on hand that were appropriate for the situation. Freezing in their furs, they awaited morning so that it would bring some light. It was no longer snowing. Under the overcast sky, D'Houtpol's heart stopped beating.

Is It Possible to Find Something without Having Any Hope?

In the Australian winter sports resort of Thredbo, a landslide buried ski instructor B. in a ski lodge. Rock debris and soil were piled six feet thick above the cavity in which he survived. Water poured into the hollow space. B. leaned on his elbow in order to keep his nose above water. 'A less fit man would not have lasted.' After the water drained away, the man was lying on frozen mud. In his cavity, he had about ten inches to move his head and about twenty inches for his legs. The buried man was able to hold out because the air in the space isolated him from the temperatures outside. He lasted for sixty-five hours.

After fifty-four hours, a fireman heard his weak shouts. Shouting back, he got a muffled reply, the fireman reported: 'I can hear you.' The buried man had given his name.

Afraid that the use of heavy machinery would trigger a further landslide, this time one fatal to the ski instructor, the helpers dug for eleven hours with their bare hands. A doctor kept up the buried man's spirits. Through a pipe he described the blue sky outside. He, the doctor, and the buried man would be able to look at this sky together that same afternoon.

First of all, the victim was supplied with warm air and liquid food through a hole which had been bored through the masses of rubble.

According to police statements, a second victim could be heard in the ruins not far from the ski instructor. The rescue teams, however, could not get closer to this spot without taking the risk of burying the ski instructor for good. The latter explained that he was worried about his wife, who at the time of the accident around midnight the previous night, had been lying beside him. He was not certain whether this second person was his wife.

The twenty-seven-year-old man was flown to the capital of Canberra by helicopter. Doctors stated that he was only slightly injured. Frostbite at the extremities.

The families of those buried complained that the rescue teams were making too little progress. The rescue operation continued on Sunday. There were fears of a sudden change in weather. Until now, the frost had stabilized the muddy soil. 'If it starts to rain, it'll get dangerous here.' The rescuers dug several tunnels to reach the place where the buried bedrooms were thought to be. They still believed they could save another victim.

In an interview with a journalist from Australian TV, the head of the rescue operation, Darwin McAllister, a man with a great deal of experience, concentrated on the concrete situation he had encountered on the spot and under stress.

—We don't hold out much more hope.

—Why not?

—Because of the cold, the duration of the cold.

—Is it possible to find anything without having any hope?

—No.

—Is the rescue work dangerous?

—Without hope, yes. As work in accordance with regulations: yes.

—What are your hopes as head of the rescue workers?

—I lay down the framework.

—And what do you decide?

—I absorb the hierarchy.

—What does that mean?

—There is nothing to decide.

—Why not?

—The important thing is for the rescuers to approach the scree slope CAUTIOUSLY. After that, they have to be lucky.

—To discover something?

—Not to be killed themselves if the mountain moves again.

—If there is a risk of that, would you withdraw the rescuers?

—At the last moment.

—Did one of the rescue workers hear something after fifty-four hours?

—Yes, a rescue worker on the third shift. He was very fresh.

—And he reported that to you immediately?

—Yes.

—Another decision by you?

—Why? I couldn't have stopped him from responding to the tapping.

—What is the decisive factor in deciding not to use any machines? Machines remove the six feet of debris in one hour, and not eleven.

—Machines would have to be driven up. They put pressure on the scree wherever you want them to be.

—Again, there's no possibility of making a decision?

—None.

—Whose idea was it to introduce the warm air and liquid food by way of tubes through the scree.

—A first-aid attendant had the idea.

—You raised no objection. To that extent, it was your decision after all?

—I don't know what you're getting at.

—Now one of the rescuers can hear sounds.

—Another buried person perhaps.

—What else could it be?

—A mistake or an animal.

—You are now sacrificing one human being for the sake of the safe rescue of another?

—I don't order anything, that's right.

—Could you have given an order?

—No.

—Are these difficult issues? Are there guidelines for such cases?

—No.

—But difficult issues?

—To the extent that I will be prosecuted for 'failure to give assistance with fatal consequences' if the buried man is killed in the end and the second buried person turns out to be a phantom.

—Could you or even should you have questioned the ski instructor who was possibly a relation of the second victim?

—Could, yes. That would have caused confusion. It's better not to make any decision.

—Was anything dug up at the location later on where the second tapping sounds were coming from?

—There were no further tapping sounds. There's not been any digging yet.

—Why not?

—We would have endangered the tunnel.

—If you don't, in fact, decide anything as the man in charge when such a catastrophe occurs, what would happen if you weren't there at all?

—A great deal. Several rescue workers would occupy my position and would perhaps try to decide something.

—Why them and not you?

—Because there would be several of them. They would compete with one another.

—Would they jockey for influence?

—That's right.

—You'd prevent that?

—Exactly.

—Are you proud of what you've done?

—Against all probability after sixty-five hours, we rescued a man from this mass of ice and scree.

—Why did that happen here and hardly ever anywhere else? Is there another word for improbability?

—We managed not to lose hope. The rescuer, not yet worn out by events, thought he could hear something; it worked like a credit on the account of hope.

—What do you mean by hope?

—Scepticism.

—Scepticism of what?

—Scepticism in the face of probability.

—At that point, you had already been on the scene for fifty-four hopeless hours. Had your hopes not been used up in the meantime? You are an *experienced* man.

—This is what I do: I don't permit myself any special thoughts.

—Curious.

—Yes. It's a matter of experience.

The Strong Influence of a Daughter

We discussed it for weeks. Berenike had always had a strong will and she had an influence over me. Herta, my wife, argued against it at first. But there wasn't a glimmer of hope. Although life as a blind person would have been no worse for Berenike than a life sentence in one of those super-prisons they're building in the States now or Homer's life during his final years. Embroiled in conversations, we didn't see that side of it.

On Sunday, Berenike lay down in bed at about 10 p.m. I bound her hands and feet with a piece of rope. She's a tall, slim girl of twenty-two. It's well known that a human being vigorously defends herself before suffocating. As agreed, Herta and I stuck adhesive tape over her mouth and nose. We sat down beside her on the bed. For a moment, she's quiet. After that, she makes violent attempts to move; her face turns red. About two minutes pass this way. She becomes motionless. I try to find her heartbeat.

Then, even though we were prepared, I was seized by an impulse (like the one we had observed in our beloved daughter a few seconds before). I tear the adhesive tape from her mouth and nose. Herta wanted to stop me. She says: A blind daughter with brain damage, that's all we need! She reminded me of what the three of us had sworn to one another. I cut the bonds with a knife. No movement of hands and feet. I called the emergency doctor.

We had discussed everything very carefully. We had never been as serious in our lives as during those days. What was to happen afterwards, what we wanted to do with our dead daughter, that was something we had not talked over. Did we want to say to our family doctor that it had been suicide or a 'natural death'? I don't know. Nor did Herta. Did my call to the emergency doctor destroy our plan? We were unable to reconstruct it. The doctor confirmed her death and was about to make out the death certificate, but then he hesitated. Outwardly, there were no signs that pointed to a *death struggle*. We waited for the police.

I would call Berenike a 'radiant creature'. After her birth, her umbilical cord cut, she lay next to Herta's bed and looked over at us. We both thought: This creature comes from another planet. I still think that today. It may be that as an engineer I shouldn't assume that, since the transport route of such a 'light of life' would be a very vague hypothesis (from one of Uranus's moons? From one of the nearby fixed stars? From a parallel world? From a time tunnel?). There are ideas in our minds that evade clarification. It was this light character on which Berenike's influence was based and which led us into this trap.

The public prosecutor was friendly. The court can be expected to be accommodating, he said, since the 'share in the crime' between myself and my wife could 'ultimately' not be determined, was split, as it were, and my impulse to tear off the adhesive tape came close to an 'abandonment of the deed, admittedly with inadequate results'.

I made no comment on that because I have quite a different problem. As clearly as I always felt the origin of our daughter to be from another star, it is just as impossible for me to imagine that the suffocated girl could survive on another star or in one of the high mountain regions of our blue planet. That *assumption* has died in me. Herta confirmed this feeling. We both don't want to live like this any more, but we can't create the impulse that kills us like we killed our daughter. The magic of the week-long three-way talks has disappeared. Prison would thus suit us better, since we wouldn't have to make any decisions of our own.

Over the winter Berenike was in hospital. After that the conversations, then came her death. We cannot go forward or back. We have let go of the therapist who spoke words of comfort to us.

Background Conversation with the Public Prosecutor (PP)

—Dr Laue, what will the indictment say?

—Manslaughter. I have no reason to doubt the statements by the father and mother about the dead woman.

—Could the daughter's illness have been cured?

—As far as we have established, no. It's retinopathia pigmentosa. The sight fades very gradually.

—Like a fade-out.

—For a while, the patient still sees something. Shadows. With luck, the patient can see as if through a very long tube. There was no such luck in the present case.

—But it's possible for a blind person to read?

—Of course. It's not the same thing as reading, but if there's nothing else. You haven't touched your coffee yet.

—Thanks. How do you explain such a collective short circuit in the family? The patient would not have committed suicide alone. Does emotional coldness or aggression play a part?

—I'm a lawyer, not a psychologist.

—But you think about the case.

—I would say: excessive devotion. The dead woman meant everything to the perpetrators. An exaggerated sensibility.

—And the dead woman makes this the vehicle of her will. She uses her influence over her parents in order to achieve death? A death obtained by sheer obstinacy?

The public prosecutor devoured the female clerk with his eyes. He was prepared to travel a long way from his professional competence and into the field of philosophy to please her. The objective limit was the rule that sexual relations with dependents and/or personnel undergoing training must be avoided. His eyes were feeling their way towards this limit. There were reserves within him (as in the ambitiously interested eyes of his young colleague) that were not needed for daily business.

If these parents who, after all, brought me into this world, said the public prosecutor, can't help me, then they should make up for that by taking my life. That was the dead woman's view. I remember that as a seven-year-old child I crouched in the skylight of the attic in my parents' house and wanted to jump from the roof to punish my parents.

CLERK. Children are vindictive?

PP. They forgive nothing.

CLERK. That's an underlying current in them?

PP. Yes, a radical current that knows only the alternative EITHER/OR.

CLERK. 'Down in one'.

PP. What's that?

CLERK. It's something one says: Bourbon cocktail down in one.

PP. It's an advertising slogan?

CLERK. No, it's text from a magazine.

PP. And what's it about?

CLERK. About abandoning yourself and about the experiences of one-night stands.

PP. Ah, I see. Hence down? And in one?

CLERK. Over and done with. The whole glass gone in one go.

PP. That's the suddenness of the feeling. The underlying current we mentioned earlier (and that is found in every one of us beneath our education in sufficient quantities that border on madness), it can only assert itself suddenly or not at all. Only, therefore, when there's a sudden lack of time.

CLERK. A rift in time . . .

PP. What?

CLERK. The thread breaks for a moment.

PP. And so in the final phase, these three never had any time. Hectic visits to the hospital. Doctors changed twice. The desperate woman brought home. Conversations under the pressure of time.

CLERK. If they had been able to wait, the three of them, they would have found the tunnel for the life of a blind person.

PP. Would you rather be blind or deaf?

CLERK. I wouldn't want to have to choose.

PP. Mute?

CLERK. There's always the erotic.

PP. And this rift in time, as you call it, is that a crack in the brain?

CLERK. It's an absolute condition of feeling. I would rather be blind than renounce the rift in one's emotions.

PP. Well, well!

CLERK. If there were an air-raid warning now, we would go down to the cellar. After the whole catastrophe, order, too, is smashed. Now something is possible that one will never forgive oneself for later on.

PP. And you think that a person can't be talked out of that? That it's more important than your sensory organs being intact?

CLERK. One doesn't have to choose.

PP. Would you say, 'Thank God'?

CLERK. The way we're talking here, no.

There was warmth and familiarity. The colours in the canteen: deplorable. The situation was 'officially fenced in' and at the same time 'tingling'. The good mood benefited the formulation of the indictment, which the PP dictated afterwards on tape. Leniency was the dominant mood.

A royal couple in a northern country had an only son. He sailed away with the ships. The ships brought back only his corpse. The Queen is too old to have any more children. The king did not want to have a younger wife. The ballad tells of a great sadness: They have lost their light. Her eyesight disappeared over the horizon. 'Lights appear extraterrestrially and fade terrestrially.'

Out of Sight, Out of Mind

> 'I'll go to you. But you'll not return to me.'
>
> Samuel, *Apocrypha*

The troop of mounted men and the waggons of the Imperial baggage train disappeared over the hills. The ruler had waved. Now he was so far away that none of those remaining behind could make out whether he was looking back or waving yet again.

The excitement of the day faded away. The concrete memory of the presence of the Emperor, who had promised to come again the following year, did not survive the winter. The Harz Mountains, which surrounded the open country, were characterized by their harsh winds; the Emperor's servants, who guarded the castle, did not stay. They were from the Piedmont and departed. At first, no one dared remove furniture or stones from the castle.

The Emperor never returned. Successors, from another house, also saw no reason to come here. The land was considered a 'rebellious backwater'.

A thread ran through the centuries: the heirs of those people, who for a few weeks in the year 1196 were so filled with the presence of the Emperor that they thought this place to be as important as Rome. What is so entrancing about the Emperor? Is it the horsemen, who surround him, or the baggage train? For a few weeks, the Emperor's palace was here, in the northern Harz, the German seat of government, the magnet of Rome. Four weeks later, it was forgotten and never returned.

Love-Struck Conspirators of a More Noble Humanity

At the wedding of Nina, Countess Stauffenberg, in Bamberg in 1933, Dr Miram, a researcher of skaldic poetry, and Kantorowicz, a member of the George Circle, sat down together in a pergola away from the others.[31] They watched a few young Reichswehr officers at the centre of the wedding party who appeared to them to be particularly animated. Perhaps also because it was hardly likely that these young men would survive a war, towards which the circumstances of the time were moving. The pair engaged in conversation were not racists. In their professions, however, they searched for exceptional strands of nobility, of a passing on of

31 The George Circle does not really have any members. Affiliation is measured informally by closeness to the master, i.e. his readiness to receive someone.

something inescapably 'aristocratic', which could counteract the mere duplication of uninteresting genes, of 'levelling'. That is what they wanted to find and, if possible, 'foster and guide' such finds. Of the day's bride and groom, they thought of the man as a possible successor of the Hohenstaufen imperial house and the young, pretty woman as a BLOOD BEARER very suited to bringing resources, BLOOD, i.e. bones and cell tissue for many generations, to the old line and spirit.

KANTOROWICZ. Do you take cream?

DR MIRAM. No.

KANTOROWICZ. I beg your pardon.

DR MIRAM. There is only *one* line of descent, which has remained free of regression right down to our own time.

KANTOROWICZ. Which is?

DR MIRAM. That of the Volsungs.

KANTOROWICZ. So Vikings then? Nothing arose in our latitudes, in Germany? Or lives now?

DR MIRAM. There may be an element of it in some Westphalian woman or in an emigrant in the United States. It's the basis of our shared assumption *that not from the middle of our land a breed, the heart* will stir. That's the SECRET GERMANY, a line of descent. That has nothing to do with race in general, but with a genotype.

KANTOROWICZ. A thread that leads to something higher?

DR MIRAM. To the people of the unbroken line. The early days never released people directly without a break, without an unspeakable war between warring peoples (shepherds) and victims (farmers). Those in the north didn't sacrifice and didn't work. They remained pure robbers.

KANTOROWICZ. Puzzling.

DR MIRAM. Why puzzling?

KANTOROWICZ. I know a few such people. I recognize them by the pupils of their eyes.

DR MIRAM. And by their temples!

KANTOROWICZ. No, by their eyes.

DR MIRAM. And the back of the head, cheek bones, gait?

KANTOROWICZ. Yes, their upright gait.

DR MIRAM. All human beings have that.

KANTOROWICZ. Yes, but a very straight, upright gait.

DR MIRAM. Nonsense. The eyes!

KANTOROWICZ. It doesn't matter. We both recognize them and would say of a couple: They are Dioscuri (if they are men), or they should have children together (if they are not of the same sex).

DR MIRAM. Assuming, of course, we recognize them.

They ordered local Franconian wine and had the coffee cleared away. The wedding celebration enlivened the afternoon.

KANTOROWICZ. I recognize them by the pupils of their eyes. Even in the 100th dilution of their origin.

DR MIRAM. Yes, yes. What worries me is that these people, whom I likewise recognize (I think I know what you mean), are usually feeble in the contemporary dilution of their blood (i.e. their blood is always more or less the same thickness as is their essence and the knowledge of their essence). They're not especially erotic or predatory, but rather lethargic.

KANTOROWICZ. I've noticed it, too. They're nevertheless noble.

DR MIRAM. Noble and lethargic.

KANTOROWICZ. Is that not a contradiction? It says in the sources: 'When the great morning breaks with fiery glow . . .'

DR MIRAM. You mean, the flash of the eyes only ignites in an emergency?

KANTOROWICZ. Yes, hence the need for an emergency.

DR MIRAM. In order to prove your preference to be correct? Even if the eyes probably perish in an emergency?

KANTOROWICZ. That would be bad.

DR MIRAM. So you really believe in it?

KANTOROWICZ. Firmly and with good reason. I am worried about something else. In antiquity in the north, there's always the same kind of behaviour (I'll go into that in more detail in my lecture in the autumn): a short-circuited action based on an impulse, a deed carried out for little reason. The last sons of Gudrun strike down their stepbrother Erp, whom immediately afterwards they desperately need for their own protection: they misunderstand his words and kill him. Sigpföti kills Högnir's servant, that's the oldest record, because he has hunted down a couple more head of game than others; he hides the dead man in the snow. The dragon's chain consists of an unstressed syllable; fate arises from unimportant things and cuts the thread of life. On the other side, lifelong, invincible devotion. They are perversely bound by oaths and fall into illegitimate love. These are the ones who unwaveringly pursue their love projects so that siblings, a great-aunt and grandson, a grandson and cousins, beget children. Inflamed in inseparable passion. Above all, the wrongly married with their brothers or sisters-in-law. Always with fatal results. The love project, the CONSTELLATION (as in the stars), survives and not the human being. Fate comes about through both, the thoughtless robbery or murder and the attraction determinable by no plan or thought.

DR MIRAM. One cannot say married. They're heathen.

KANTOROWICZ. I also talk about 'constellations'. A depressive basic position, that's what I mean.

DR MIRAM. Is it not what your master calls your CORROSIVE VIEW OF THINGS?

KANTOROWICZ. No, no. I share the sustained longing of those people, on whom the ancient texts report. Just as I hope for the return of the king. Perhaps we shall see one at this celebration?

DR MIRAM. Yes. He is a ruler.

KANTOROWICZ. Yes.

They both look at the young Stauffenberg.

DR MIRAM. I take that back about the Jewish 'corrosion'. Aisthanomai = to perceive; lüein = to dissolve. That's the Aislü type. That's what you are, my friend. By virtue of your Jewish character. In the event there is no last circle of the noble to be found on earth, you want to use scepticism as a way out. Where there's nothing to love, you pass by, do you not?

KANTOROWICZ. Could it be borne otherwise?

DR MIRAM. If it's not there?

KANTOROWICZ. If it could not exist anywhere?

DR MIRAM. So it's only about something that lies beyond all horizons.

KANTOROWICZ. Yes, that's certainly where it lies. It lives there prominently.

DR MIRAM. But with the necessary fateful outcome. Then it would be better not to keep a look-out for it? To appear sluggish?

KANTOROWICZ. That is not true of the women who possess such pupils.

DR MIRAM. You mean the eyes that are described in the texts?

KANTOROWICZ. Exactly. They are also mentioned in the case of Frederick II, Holy Roman Emperor, and I know them. I have already seen them myself.

DR MIRAM. But never deeds that were conspicuous?

KANTOROWICZ. No, not that. But the eyes . . .

It was growing dark. A child that had fallen into the river was pulled out by young officers. Punch was passed round.

DR MIRAM. Not all of them died. You know the daughter of the union of Brunhilde with Sigurd, a strange text?

KANTOROWICZ. Aslang, who calls herself Kraka.

DR MIRAM. That is where these eyes come from today. There is no other line but that.

KANTOROWICZ. There must be a second source of aristocracy: The children Jesus had with Mary Magdalene; immediately after the death of Jesus they were taken to Marseilles. The Cathars maintained there was a line of succession, and I have heard that Obersturmführer Rahn is researching it.

DR MIRAM. What a repulsive idea.

KANTOROWICZ. The spirit, if you would care to listen to me for another moment, can be transmitted by others apart from the Norsemen bodies. Kingship, too, cannot be handed down only by the Vikings.

DR MIRAM. Yes. There's the Stauffenberg way.

KANTOROWICZ. And if one wants to breed people back in the same way as thoroughbred horses, do you have in mind to SET A NEW MAN AGAINST American mass society and the Strength-through-Joy masses of Europe (including the French consumer character), always in the hope that the eyes, which enchant you, really are also bearers of spiritual values and not good-looking zeros?

DR MIRAM. You are expressing yourself very coarsely. That tells me you are depressed.

KANTOROWICZ. You would have to be a brothel keeper and not a university teacher and skaldic researcher to have the necessary run of people in order to find and to match-make your SELECT BAND. Brangaine wears a Jewish-masculine dress.

DR MIRAM. If you were not curious, you would not argue so coarsely.

Champagne was now served instead of Franconian wine and punch. The two bards would have liked nothing better than to act as match-makers to the young men at this wedding celebration. They would have raised the resulting children and crossed them again until a human race grew up, *as the gardens glow*.

But to do that, it's necessary to isolate cells capable of reproduction in test tubes and let these vials (in sheer memory of unforgettable, promising pairs of eyes) copulate; from such alchemy, an avenging noble band is released, a HEART OF THE WORLD and meanwhile all the rest are killed. Max Kommerell, another companion with whom Kantorowicz had a conversation a week later, said that. It was, however, doubtful, as Kantorowicz conceded to his friend, whether such a collection of chance findings was worthwhile. He never got to know people who possessed such pupils more than fleetingly. Was it not possible, rather, that the opposite path could also promise success? Namely, the 'child of man as a blank sheet'; orphans from Rio de Janeiro or illiterates from numerous nameless lines of descent who know nothing of the past and never knew anything either. And these wretched, empty hearts could be filled with culture. Perhaps this would be the beginning of the NEW HUMAN at the opposite pole of descent, at the end of all the mixing?

Night had descended. Large sparks and small lights were everywhere in the heavens. The conspirators talked themselves into an irreducible anticipation. They wanted to make it to the profession of SEER. Kantorowicz was certain that he would get through the autumn semester at the University of Frankfurt, indeed, he could turn it into a success by amazing his students. In December, the National Socialist disruption would take full effect; at Christmas, he would arrive in Oxford, where he would occupy a safe OBSERVATION TOWER (like Lynceus) for the coming war. He is the discoverer of 'secret Germany'. He coined the term REBIRTH for Germany, even if not for nationalist reasons, because this land can forever not be a nation and none of the GREAT GERMAN CAESARS ever thought nationally.

What this circle of CONSPIRATORS IN LOVE WITH A MORE NOBLE HUMANITY (in continuation of Goethe, Napoleon I, Hölderlin, Nietzsche, OBEDIENT to the Master Stefan George) did not accomplish in practice was the REFOUNDATION OF THE HUMAN RACE.

Only the George Circle, whose Jewish members had all left the country by the end of 1933, had a poetically unrefuted conception of LEADING MANKIND OUT OF ITS MISERY BY ENNOBLING IT. The Master had crossed Lake Constance. Whether that was to be understood as going into exile in Switzerland or as a holiday, only the dead man can say. By autumn, he lay ill in Misox in the Ticino. On 6 December 1933, his faithful followers buried him in foreign soil.

On that day when so many orders were given by responsible officers without full authority (and many of them were carried out), a sergeant brought five corpses, four officers and a civilian, under cover of falling darkness. He told the cemetery keeper he received an order to bury the five corpses, to heap earth on them. He requested a spade to start the burial.

Frightened by the events of the day that he followed on the radio, the cemetery keeper, however, did not feel he was covered until he called in the commander of the local police station. So the three of them stood in front of the five corpses, which the sergeant had brought down from the truck and laid on a cemetery barrow.

No one assumed that the sergeant had murdered the five and now wanted to hide them in the only spot where they wouldn't be conspicuous. It seemed much more credible that he was acting under orders (he had come from the War Ministry at the Bendler Building, his identification described him as attached to the ministry). More competent authorities had the five corpses on their conscience. Nevertheless, the idea of burying them without presentation of a document or of a death certificate did not inspire confidence.

Finally, the station commander brought in some of his men who helped the sergeant excavate a provisional grave. There was no other choice but this provisional procedure so that the dead had earth on their faces.

FIGURE 8. Pirates seizing a merchant ship on the Black Sea on 25 October 1929. Because none of the armed intruders spoke a word, their nationality could not be established. The steamer was looted. The perpetrators were whisked away by an aeroplane. This suggests radio communications were behind the crime.

FIGURE 9. Police protection on Wall Street during the stock-market crash. After a boom, which has lasted since 1923, there follows, on 24 October 1929, the collapse, which we call 'Black Friday' in Europe.

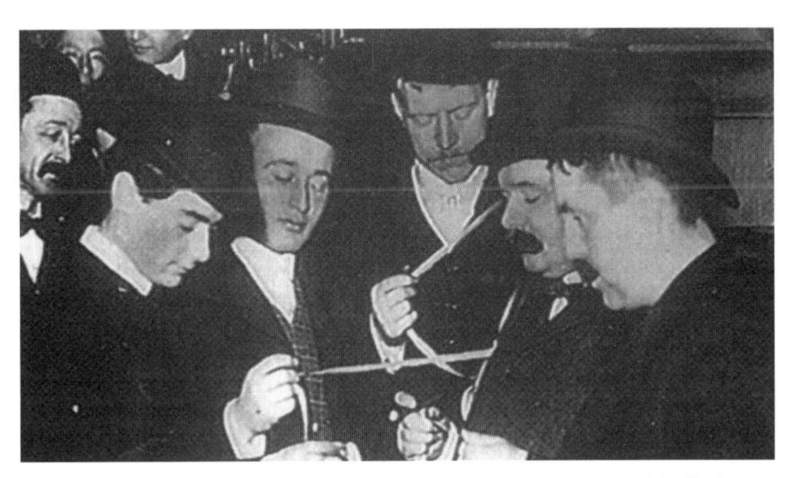

FIGURE 10. Principles of life on Black Friday: Don't run in the corridors of the Exchange, don't curse, always have a joke ready, your facial expression should be inscrutable.

TIDE IS TURNED WITH QUICK AID OF FINANCIERS. Friday, 25 October, shortly before the end of trading. On behalf of J. P. Morgan & Co, John McGouldzick goes up to the counter of United Steel and buys at the previous day's price. BUYING ORDERS GIVEN AS ISSUES TUMBLE HALT SELLING FLOOD. The exchange falters and in the last fifteen minutes of the day it turns into a bull market.

FIGURE 11. On Tuesday, 29 October, there follows another crash, one worse than that on Thursday or Friday of the previous week. On Friday, bankers bought, now they sell secretly. The breach of confidence triggers a panic on Tuesday. In all, 16,410,030 shares are traded.

FIGURE 12. Dr Gerd Ziehlke, GDR economist (ret.), analyses two causes of September 1929, which, hardly noticed at the time, can be recognized as triggers of the fall:

1. The refusal of the Massachusetts Public Service Commission to allow Boston Edison Company to split its shares.
2. The collapse of a fund which relied on International Combustion Engineering shares.

These two causal chains have only really been discovered now, with a delay of sixty years, by Ziehlke and have been named after him ('the Ziehlke effect').

FIGURE 13. A storm on Lake Michigan. Seven ships sank in the period between 24 and 30 October 1929. On 30 October, the Coast Guard rescued forty-three survivors of the *Wisconsin*. Captain Douglas Morrison, First Officer Edward Helvordson and Quartermaster William Stanheim were last seen injured and at the bow of the ship before it sank. They and thirty-five passengers were lost.

Principles of Life on Black Friday, II

NO 'HUMAN' UNDERSTANDING

'I don't do anything out of nervousness,' that was Dr Söhnlein's principle in case of danger. Latin American stocks were falling, European stocks were following the rough and tumble lead of Wall Street, in Australia, in Hong Kong. Tokyo was lost. Vienna and Stockholm held up until midday, then they fell. The chorus of share prices in Hungary and Berlin sang a dirge. Someone who, his eyes wide open, loses a fortune entrusted to him must bear this with 'imperturbable calm'. It's unusual for someone to shoot himself.

The only thing a human being can do in such an extreme case when they lose all their fortune and trust is to sit tight.

The advantage of catastrophes at sea is that in being driven forward by the wind, the steamer or sailing ship will not encounter, in all likelihood, any obstacle and that the storm will certainly die down after a while (for human circumstances that's often too late). The image of a stock-exchange crash, on the other hand, says Dr Söhnlein, corresponds more to what happens when the bow of a modern warship is struck by a rocket, and the vessel, with the tremendous HP dynamic built into it dives below the surface of the water and plunges towards the centre of the earth. At a certain depth, the cruiser will burst apart, the individual bits will decelerate at less than 1 g and begin to sink to the seabed. It is a calm picture, an illustration of the sentence: 'Don't display any nervousness'.

Only seven big speculators—for moments at a time, they are capable of joining together in hunting teams and seldom act against one another (like the GNOMES OF ZURICH)—are in a position to plan raids and carry them through according to plan. Everyone who is smaller than them will avoid movement.

On a day at the beginning of July (one can't say 'on a hot day' in accordance with impressions at the London stock exchange since a global context is at stake and it was hot in Chicago, cooler in Stockholm, very cold on the Kerguelen Islands), four entrepreneurs set a trap with the support of two pension funds and Arab money. Tellus, the spinning globe, forced Sydney, Tokyo, Hong Kong to show their hands first in the global game of poker. They constituted a future that only reached the exchanges of Frankfurt and London ten hours later and New York's sixteen hours later. Three hours after that, the 'Executioners of Chicago' struck and responded to the arbitrary opening prices in the Far East. Whole industries were gnawed down to skin and bone and, knowing that the hunters were lying in wait, were forced to publish new offerings the next morning local time. The hackers on the dark side of the globe slept.

THE FORGOTTEN COMPANY

In the midst of the fall in prices on Black Friday in the year 1929, the share value of a joint-stock company called Phönix & Agros AG held up without any notice. The company appeared to own land in Cyprus and operated alchemical workshops in Aleppo where top-quality wines were replicated in chemical laboratories; it had also produced plans for popular drinks that were to come on the market by the mid-century.

Whether in October 1929 anyone was still working on the tasks set out in the company prospectus, we do not know. The company's business was administered in trust by a lawyer's office in Athens. The majority of shares were owned by dispossessed southern Russian noble families and an insurance company forced to liquidate in the Soviet Union; the aristocrats were regarded as lost without trace. These shareholders kept quiet. No one enquired about the shares or sold even one. Until 1932, the price of this stock consistently remained at the same level on 4

September 1929, a lonely peak. When an analyst bought some assets as a test and then wanted to resell them, this PILLAR OF THE OLD WORLD also collapsed.

A MATTER OF FAITH

In Hong Kong (after the takeover of the Crown Colony in 1999), Chinese secret service officers found in the cellars of the stock exchange a room, in which religious utensils, pictures of saints, trinkets and candles were kept. They were arranged in the manner of a 'European place of devotion or a chapel' and there was room for fifteen worshippers, assuming they pressed themselves close together like people seeking refuge in an air-raid shelter. Did a secret society of Christian stock exchange magnates steer world developments from here? Through conspiracies?

The deputy commander of the reconnoitring unit, a specialist in currency movements and economic crime, saw his view confirmed that 'stock-exchange reality' (at the time, a view favoured by a government tending to opportunism) was a sectarian religious movement. It was possible to distinguish Asian, Christian, Islamic, animistic share price developments. This was, however, impossible, the officer thought, because the sectarian religious practices that regulated the tremendous overvaluation or destruction of stock exchange assets went under different names and were differently constituted in every country.

The ritual objects discovered in the stock exchange building were confiscated. They proved to be of little value, trinkets. An announcement was prepared, the security guards and the management of the exchange were warned. In the days that followed, all Asian prices fell. The Chinese leadership, superstitious and already long dependent on the mysterious meteorological manifestations of the international market, had the confiscated religious showpieces brought out of the depot, where they were waiting to be auctioned off, and then piled them up in empty rooms in the stock exchange, this time on the twenty-sixth floor. None of the believers who set up the cult hide-out (or, if you will, free enterprise booster) in the cellars found what had been piled up on the twenty-sixth floor, and thus no concentrated prayers or incantations could manipulate the flow of worldwide faith. Prices plummeted.

FIGURE 14

AS LONG AS THE SHEET MUSIC LASTS

It is not well known that the bow of the TITANIC dived so quickly into the icy waters that in the saloons an air bubble held for a considerable amount of time. In it (i.e. in a ball of 300 cubic metres of compressed oxygen) the ship's orchestra played from the sheet music brought from Southampton until five o'clock in the morning. Certainly, they weren't playing for wages any more, nor out of loyalty to the owners or the captain, with whom all contact had broken off. They played medleys because any change in what they did would have driven them to despair. What else should they do when they suspected after all that the water was lurking at every exit of the brilliantly illuminated saloon?

The ship reached the seabed at about 3 a.m. It skidded across a sandy dune and came to a halt at the bottom of a valley. The musicians felt the impact as a jolt and the lack of motion (for 100 years or more, because the raising of the *Titanic* is still uncertain) as UNEASE. For the first time in days: they weren't going anywhere. The background noise (gurgling, sirens, the sound of the boilers, cries of those who wanted to be saved)—which they had battled against with their foxtrots, operetta melodies and tango tunes—all that was gone. There was an acoustic not often available to players of light music, one inaudible, however, to the musicians who couldn't hear themselves but who now played on in the face of the hopelessness of the situation. For no other reason than that, any change in their activity would only have further increased their inner unease.

FIGURE 15. A 5 per cent increase in telephone conversations by the Transatlantic Cable during the crisis. The turnover of the Western Union Telegraph Company increases by this amount. The shareholder value of the enterprise contracts by 54 per cent.

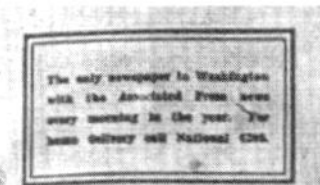

The Washington Post.

NO. 19,489. WASHINGTON: FRIDAY, OCTOBER 25, 1929. THREE CENTS

BANKERS ACT TO CURB STOCK PANIC

…LL VERDICT …AY BE GIVEN …Y JURY TODAY

…el Locked Up Last Night on Failure to Decide.

…RT TO BE OPENED …T 10 THIS MORNING

…enys and Daughters …f Accused Wait in Vain Decision.

…MER SECRETARY REMAINS AT HOTEL

…se Counsel in Object… …n to Charge Outlined by Justice Hitz.

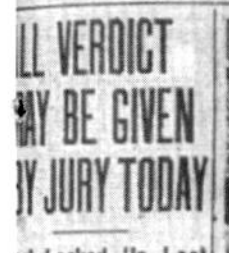

DEFENDS LOBBY

GRUNDY ADMITS AID IN TARIFF FRAMING

Pennsylvanian Says He Has Been Working for High Rates Since 1897.

SEES DUTY TO PLATFORM

POLICE FORCE TUG-O'-WAR IS GIVEN SACKETT

Capper Sheds Blease's Resolution on Pratt With Alacrity.

DOYLE AND ALLEN HIRE ATTORNEYS FOR TRIAL

Formal Charges to Be Completed by Clerk, Probably Today.

ALLEN PLAYS ANOTHER TRUMP AS DETECTIVE

Private Has Brand New Case to Be Investigated by District Attorney.

TIDE IS TURNED WITH QUICK AID OF FINANCIERS

Buying Orders Given as Issues Tumble Halt Selling Flood.

CALM VIEW IS TAKEN AT LEADERS' PARLEY

Dignified Reassurance Is Extended in Midst of Buzz of Rumors.

COURAGE RETURNS WHEN SHORTS COVER

Upturn, However, Fails to Restore Losses That Created Hysteria.

BANK HEADS CONFER ON STOCKS' DEBACLE

GOVERNMENT CALM IN STOCK RAMPAGE

Commerce Agencies Find No Need for Action; Reserve Board Meets Twice.

GENERAL BUSINESS SAFE

WALL STREET HUMS WITH NIGHT TOILERS

Entire Office Staffs Ordered to Work Right Through Until Morning.

CANYON LIGHTS SHINING

SALES RECORD IS SET WHILE PRICES CRAS…

Hurl 12,894,650 Share… Overboard as Wild Scenes Occur.

BROKERS COLLAPSE ON EXCHANGE FLOO…

Uproar Heard for Blocks Attracting Big Crowd to Building.

TUMULT GREATEST IN SECURITY HISTOR…

Bears Reap Millions Whi… Scores of Issues Drop $15 to $70 Each.

FIGURE 16. Powerful bankers. W. C. Potter (left), Charles E. Mitchell (middle), Thomas W. Lamont (right). Accompanied by film cameras, they meet for talks in the building of the J. P. Morgan & Co. Bank. The fact that they are sitting down together is newsworthy. The seriousness of the situation can be measured by the length of the meeting.

FIGURE 17. A mechanical ticker. It's capable of putting out 231 numerals or letters per minute. During the extreme challenge of Black Friday (turnover fourteen million shares), it registers a delay of one to two hours after a result. The fact that it is impossible for investors and brokers to know what their orders and results are worth at any moment adds to their nervousness. Charles P. Kindleberger and J. K. Galbraith consider this time dysfunction to be the decisive factor. Panic breaks out because events happen too quickly and simultaneously time measurement isn't working.

FIGURE 18. On Friday, 25 October, Richard Whitney, president of the New York Exchange, halts trading at 2.57 p.m. His bell interrupts euphoric shouting and a series of offers. In the last quarter of an hour there had been a rally. The low prices aroused greed.

Like a besieged town in the Middle Ages, Kindleberger writes, which throws food to its enemy in order to unnerve them, Richard Whitney shuts down the exchange three minutes early and, in expectation of a boom on Monday morning, wastes a number of valuable offers. His quick-witted behaviour creates a news item that immediately crosses the Atlantic.

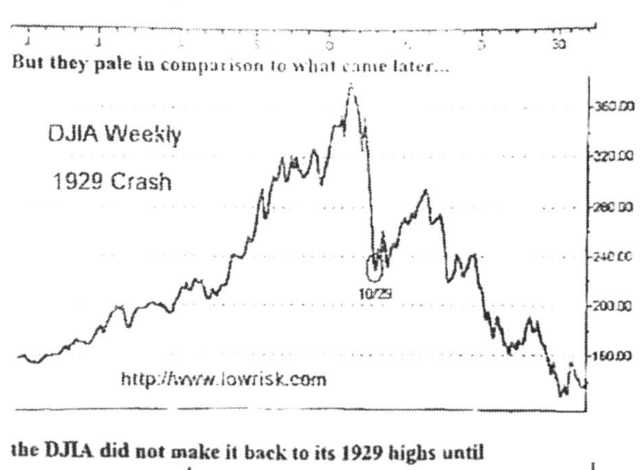

FIGURE 19. The Dow Jones shows the crashes on Thursday the 24th and Tuesday the 29th of October, BLOODY TUESDAY. The failure of the market principle, writes Charles P. Kindleberger, is demonstrated in the years 1930, 1931, 1932. The public impression, however, has settled on the first news of the failure in October 1929.[32]

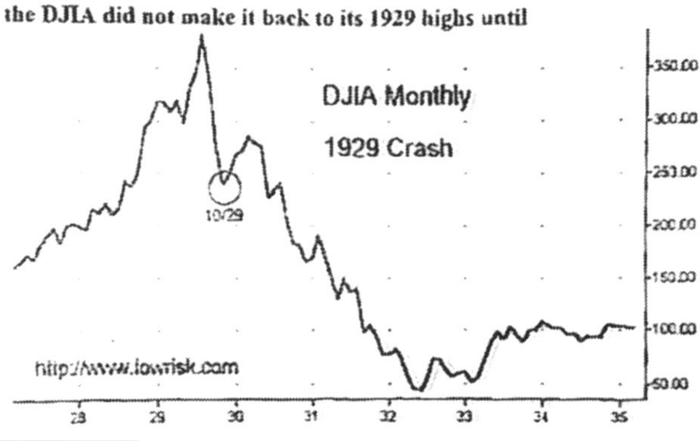

FIGURE 20. In the monthly Dow Jones report, whose curve here represents the years 1928–1935, one can see, says Kindleberger, that the low of October 1929 is modest compared with the lows of 1932 to 1933.

32 Charles P. Kindleberger, *The World in Depression, 1929–1939* (Berkeley: University of California Press, 1986).

FIGURE 21. Abraham Germansky, a real-estate stock-exchange dealer from 140 East Broadway, New York City, disappears on the Thursday. No one ever hears from him again. After the stock-exchange crash, he is seen on Broadway looking at ticker tabs. Friends and relatives say he was unable to bear the loss of considerable sums. The loss had attacked his reason.

OBITUARY

The broker Adolf Krüger, resident at 42 Kaiserstraße in Halberstadt, first ate breakfast in the Grand Hotel Leopold I in Brussels and then shot himself on the balcony of his hotel room so that the gun smoke, which he imagined would be worse than it actually was, did not alter the suite's elegant interior. Passers-by stood still because of the sound of the shot and saw a tall man collapse.

A bellboy brought news from the stock market in exchange for no tip; in fact, no one opened to his insistent knocking, and he took the note about the losses to the reception, where, because of the excitement that had broken out, no one accepted the information. Doctors and police arrived. The final deficit, which decided on Krüger's fortune, remained 'lost'.

The dead man didn't need the notice of his losses. He knew from the *trend* in prices that he no longer had a chance, neither in his profession nor in this world. At stake is money entrusted to him. He had no knowledge of Latin and knew nothing of the custom of generals to fall on their swords after a lost battle. Without a conscious role model, he remained loyal to a long series of reliable people in charge.

THE WEASEL

Called 'the weasel' and known for his strong nerves, Klaus Löhlein bought the cheapest blue-chip stocks on behalf of Russian emigres who deposited jewels for a credit they required (they also persuaded aristocratic relatives from the West to take out mortgages on their lands in Hungary, Czechoslovakia and Silesia); these registered shares entitled them entry into valuable, but at present underrated factories. Banks and real estate were among them, associated with extensive production holdings, which the Weasel 'gutted' and chewed to pieces like bits of sausage; they were linked to other valuables by way of exchanges in kind. With patience and the ability to retain the trust of his customers with the company, he built an empire in two years that secured the existence of his customers until 1944. The investment was paid back in January 1934.

In no way did the Weasel proceed according to the observable stock-market prices. Instead, he had detectives investigate the invisible value of the original objects that denoted the shares. No one else on the stock exchange did that. The most invisible item, the reserves, says the Weasel, corresponds to 'the fat on the back of a goose'.

Löhlein owed his nickname, the *weasel*, to his apparently swift ability to come to decisions (he was a patient listener every time his detectives gave long reports), the particular way he moved along the corridors of his Antwerp hotel and the sudden relocation of his headquarters, which made him seem omnipresent (he was anything but quick and more like a midwife than a killing beast). Furthermore, he didn't eat meat, not even on high holy days; he was thrifty, as his forefathers from Odessa commanded. He never took more than 5 per cent on a 'successful deal'. Losses were borne at the expense of the house.

THE CORPSE OF A COWARD

After the loss of his own fortune and the inheritance of Prince Yussopov, which had been entrusted to him, Erwin Lewinsky fled to a lake in Mecklenburg. The prince's huntsman tracked him down there and shot him with a Browning revolver. He threw the body in a sewer. Because the lake was too good 'for the corpse of a coward'.

As a hacker on the Internet (we call ourselves 'radio operators'), I don't need to fear bankers in Hong Kong, Frankfurt am Main, Zurich or Chicago, as far as the competency of the stock exchange is concerned. Aside from the fact that events at the world's exchanges, when seen electronically, take place at such high speeds that the management organs of capital can't follow them in real time. Young people at their monitors like us, however, are at least *almost* in sync with our perceptions and forecasts. We have acquired our competency from disappointment.[33]

The original source of our disappointment: Calls in June 1990 for help from the Elbe Shipyard, a former East German nationally owned enterprise in Werdau. We knew the yard from our internships. There were four of us: a dramaturge, an engineer, an economist, an editor. We were all Marxists at the top of our class.[34]

We were UNPREPARED. Yes, we had an analysis of the current complicated situation in the GDR. Both the liquidation of our industries and the introduction of the D-mark were together a pledge of the VICTORY OF FINANCE CAPITAL OVER PRODUCTION CAPITAL. Put another way: the chain of events belongs to the PERMANENCE OF PRIMITIVE ACCUMULATION. The voracious appetite of capital repeats the primitive expropriation that preceded the Peasant Wars. A chain of political consequences can be drawn from such an analysis.[35] We were not quick enough, however, in drawing up the opening balance sheet of the Elbe Shipyard. It was not ready within the period

33 The present author, Fred Walhasch from East Berlin, has brought in considerable stock-exchange winnings for his collective in the last two years.

34 Marxism cannot be one's chief profession. In this respect, Marx, too, says of himself that he is not a Marxist.

35 The Trotskyist T. Gurland and the Cuban economist Gonzales confirm our collectively worked-out theses as correct.

stipulated. What's more, everything we had taken into the balance sheet as cover for this national property was wrong.[36]

As a Marxist without hope of a permanent position, I, Fred Walhasch, live like young Marx himself. Nobody wants me. I write articles for foreign newspapers and put together dossiers.

What trouble we took to prepare ourselves for an emergency! The study of Marxism requires seven years of practical experience and seven years of study; it is unto itself a task of a lifetime.[37]

Now, Fred Walhasch continues in his report, Victor and I share our female companions, but we comply with what they want of their own accord. Female and male communities are among the early sources of Marxism. On the Internet, we are linked up to what's happening on the stock exchanges. For example, we order CHINA STAR in the early morning; yesterday it was forty-nine cents, today it's ten cents. The drop in stock prices affecting all Asian shares is a result of Chinese threats against Taiwan.[38] To what extent, the theatre director Frank

---

36 The real estate would have to have been separated out in the form of a limited company; step by step against a loan obligation of this company to the nationally owned enterprise or VEB, at the same level as the central credit obligation of the VEB to the Central Bank, which now passed to the Finance Ministry of the Federal Republic. There was a way out! If only we had seen it in time!

37 The chronological outline of the effort is still abbreviated in somewhat illusory fashion here. Yes, the problem of LIVING MARXISM is that it is impossible for an individual, whether in practical work or as a theorist, to appropriate Marxist theory as a single person. Sixteen generations of devoted, active bearers of ideas—always with a relation to practice and also always oriented, therefore, towards the practice of the enemy—would be just about sufficient to sustain a GRUNDRISS, i.e. an OUTLINE OF MARXISM. The process itself, that is PROGRESS, requires seven emigrations and a time span of 112 generations.

38 The course of history is never logical. Two days later, our analytical approach triumphs; Pacific Century Cyber Works, China Star and Founder, our 'race horses', rise. We started out with our severance pay of 17,800 DM per person and we are now millionaires.

Castorf asks me, are you 'without hope' given the great success of your business activity? As a Marxist, Fred Walhasch replied, I am without hope for the foreseeable future because in the company of so many others I stand ALONGSIDE THE PRODUCTION PROCESS as if it were not my life. While in this position, I make a profit. Something like that is practical, but it still doesn't make a Marxist hopeful.

THE CLOSE OF THE MARKET

In a hut, Major General von Kehr listened to the offers made by the local Macedonian ruling power. The man was a representative of the Greek king; he knew Paris, Brussels, London and Rome. He had at his disposal six sergeants from the Royal Greek Army and a few irregulars, estate owners practised in the use of hunting weapons. They offered the German general permanent residence, all the civil rights of the province, as many officers and men in his troops as workers or servants as he wanted, landed property the size of a German manor (or more).[39] The officers of his staff and the unit commanders, up to the rank of major, were also to receive an estate, as was once, said the local ruler Count Dürkheim Gregorevich, victorious Roman legions were once entitled to. Condition: the German division must remain until the region had been pacified, i.e. the rural population intimidated, Communist infiltrators eliminated and certain areas taken away from the neighbouring province. Renaming the province an autonomous republic and thereby founding a state, said the local ruler, might be possible.

39 The Russian breakthrough in eastern Poland in the winter of 1945 made the withdrawal of the German troops in the Balkans, known as Army Group F, necessary. In forced marches the units crossed northern Greece, Macedonia, Yugoslavia and made for Vienna. Their vehicles had been captured from the enemy, their arms were identical with the victorious arms of 1941.

—What do the English say to it all?

It turned out that such a separation had been agreed upon with a British secret service officer. Prerequisite: the Republic was to be thought of as a buffer against the anticipated onslaught of Soviet agents and Yugoslav partisans from the north.

There was also talk of marrying into a powerful family that dominated the province. Major General von Kehr discussed the unexpected situation with his First General Staff Officer. For a moment—in this hopeless situation of the Reich and the military profession, in anticipation of certain death if the march continued—the officers deliberated. A residual amount of their skills, a material value of their force that had already been written off, could be realized in this form.

For three leaves now, von Kehr had been estranged from his wife. He could manage without his two children, if he at least knew that they did not need his help (help of a dead man, at best a man without a profession). He could beget new children with one of the local women whose passport photo had been placed before him. He believed he would be able to explain the situation to the men, whom he had led here. They would all retire from the German Reich indefinitely.

The decision was far too unusual. After so many years of military habits, they couldn't make up their minds to become founders of a state, to realize their value themselves. That was a mistake. After rejecting the elegant local offer and after an arduous 125-mile northward march, the division was completely destroyed on a mountain pass. Major General von Kehr and his staff were given a sham trial and shot by partisans. Their valueless bodies were carelessly covered with earth.

Torch of Freedom

What Is a Commodity Fetish?

In the festival events of the Great French Revolution, produced by the stage designer David, it is called the TORCH OF FREEDOM; over the centuries, within the actual people of Western Europe, it is a glowing light or ember;[40] one can also say: a rebelliousness suited to various uses. The new INNER LIGHT—is it a RELIGIOUS FOUNTAIN OF YOUTH? Perhaps altogether a divine spark? It's the seat of the compulsion to save, of industriousness, of wealth creation. Want and oppression never extinguish this light. It is, rather, *fanned* by external force. If it becomes a torch, then this affront is immediately bloodily suppressed. To that extent, no polity has any experience with how human beings could survive as TORCHES OF FREEDOM. The torch of freedom, as it is displayed at public meetings or borne in the hand of a statue, is only an image.

Suddenly, 200 years after the 'invention of freedom', it turns out that all objects that human beings exchange with one another contain an illumination. The exchange value shines as a picture or plan like conscience once did before it.

Antonio Gutierrez-Fernandez, president of the Academy in Havana, intends to use this reference to begin his lecture before the Central Committee. The small circle of defenders of the Republic meets once a week to listen to elevating lectures. The root of the revolutionary upheaval in Cuba was outright indignation at the regime of the dictator Batista: blazing. In order, however, to produce the 'passionate steadfastness', such as the republican defence of Cuba demanded, a second spark had to be discovered, an expectation of salvation, a glowing light that is independent of the presence of a tyrant. The Spanish, says Antonio

---

40 Often confused with the light of the soul.

Gutierrez-Fernandez in his lecture, bring a EUROPEAN STRUCTURE to the island, but in pre-industrial form. It contains no light as such. Some ideas of property and revenge, certainly. They import slaves, they exterminate the island's original inhabitants.

How the light of the soul of the Cubans functions cannot be explained by examples from Karl Marx. But such an INNER LIGHT has been demonstrably measured. Otherwise, Cuba (as the sole socialist country apart from the People's Republic of China, whose Marxist character is unclear) could not continue to exist. Gutierrez-Fernandez contradicts the thesis that the Cubans are an EASILY INFLAMED NATION. It is, rather, that a glowing light or a lamp of the soul shines in every human being (yet another aura shines at a short distance from the skin and all around it). These phenomena of light, which Gutierrez-Fernandez calls ORIENTATION LIGHTS, are, however, hidden by the billions of sparks in commodities, which will also flood Cuba as soon as the republican defence breaks down. Evidently lit by people, the little lights that indicate commodity value like candles on the graves of dead labour, hide the INNER light; hence, it tends to be more visible in years of shortage and times of need.

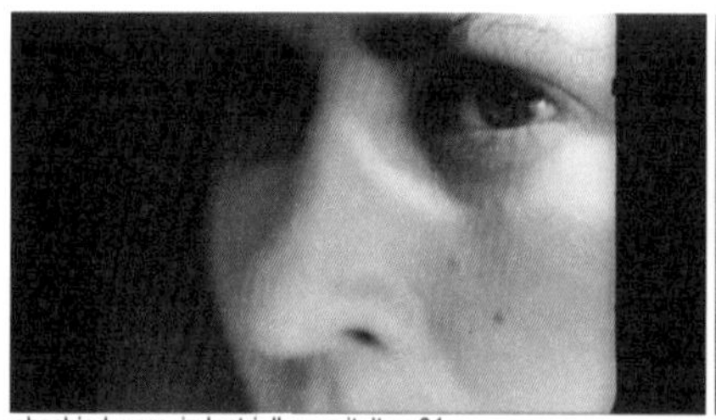
abschied_vom_industriellen_zeitalter_01

abschied_vom_industriellen_zeitalter_02

abschied_vom_industriellen_zeitalter_03

abschied_vom_industriellen_zeitalter_04

abschied_vom_industriellen_zeitalter_05

abschied_vom_industriellen_zeitalter_06

abschied_vom_industriellen_zeitalter_07

abschied_vom_industriellen_zeitalter_08

FIGURE 22

abschied_vom_industriellen_zeitalter_09
abschied_vom_industriellen_zeitalter_10
abschied_vom_industriellen_zeitalter_11
abschied_vom_industriellen_zeitalter_12
abschied_vom_industriellen_zeitalter_13
abschied_vom_industriellen_zeitalter_14

FIGURE 23

FIGURE 24

FIGURE 25

FIGURE 26

FIGURE 27

FIGURE 28

That Was the Farewell to the Industrial Age

At about midday on 30 October, even the greediest looters who were buying stock for 12 cents, which yesterday was still quoted at $138 per share, let go of this booty. It now seemed to be settled that further selling was out of the question, that the values lay buried once again in the real relations, as if there had never been a stock-exchange value. These experienced speculators acted correctly, because no more than three years later, in June 1932, rock bottom was reached. What Spark, Stephan & Co. had bought for 12 cents, one could get for 16 cents. The machinery was obsolete through lack of use.

On 30 October 1929, they were waiting with the Second International Section of the Central Committee for the telegrams that reviewed the course of events on the New York Stock Exchange. Chests of Siberian gold were transported to the loading ramps of the Kremlin; next to them, piled-up cardboard boxes, in which forty large emeralds were packed in cotton wool. Pushed together on pallets, these boxes bore inspection seals. Each box contained exactly the same weight of stones from the Ural Mountains, objects that represented in an extraordinary way the perspective of equality (each emerald is extremely distinctive and of a different size, but the sorting process created equals; the result of experts knowledgeable of ancient emerald examination techniques).

The idea of the commissars in charge, they were from Baku, was based on the fact that the crisis of belief, which had gripped the capitalist continents, didn't include the Fatherland of Working People. At the same time, however, one-fifth of the articles of value in the world were stored in the state territory of the workers and peasants. That was the estimated value. Now there was the opportunity to buy up the shattered West.

—And here are the boxes with Baku Oil shares. Seven chests with Maria-Theresia dollars. Antiques and confiscated Turkish pounds.

—We could also have property options in Siberian land printed.

They scraped together whatever could be considered a commodity value in the disturbed centres of capital; they very much wanted to feed this illusion. Since the true value did not lie hidden in commodities after all, but rather in labour power, the good will of millions of Soviet citizens. If they succeeded in pouring this value into the empty, now hopeless factories of the West and Asia's cities, that would be to REVOLUTIONIZE THE CAPITALIST REVOLUTION. There remained the language problem. The factory workers of the Soviet industrial centres are also used to different screws and machinery than what the workers of the West know.

Representatives of the Soviet government were thus dispatched to the metropoles of the West. There, they were arrested as spies as they attempted to buy up companies.

In the town of Uralsk, engineer Vladimir Putlov watched a convoy of trucks move off, on which the technical equipment from his building site, a transportable-model-building enterprise, was being removed. The machinery was to be concentrated in the capital and used to equip the project WORLD ACQUISITION, as soon as the foreign stock exchanges had been taken over. Replacements for the equipment were promised by spring. The plans for the construction of the Siberian plant on the slopes of the Ural Mountains, described three years later as obsolete, could not be carried out without the transferred machinery; seventeen years later they were liquidated altogether.

Yet the picture of the convoy driving down the muddy track to the hills and disappearing westwards never left engineer Putlov. It was, he writes in Appendix 2 of *Interviews with Veteran*

Technician by the Russian Academy of the Sciences (February 2000), THE FAREWELL TO THE INDUSTRIALIZATION OF RUSSIA. The heavy equipment was gone.

The takeover of world markets by the workers' block in late autumn 1929 was a failure. The USSR had at its disposal perhaps 800 activists who would have had experience of exchanging commodity values for share ownership in the West. A further six million talented individuals who could have moved into the workplaces of the conquered West, although residents in the country and waiting for a miracle, could not be reached by the government.

The Commissars from Baku well knew that a seizure of power by socialism with Mauser pistols, armoured trains and men was impossible. The prediction, however, that capitalists (in serious difficulties) would offer for sale the rope with which they could be hanged turned out not to be true either. Instead, the guardians of capital proved that they 'held on tenaciously', especially in a crisis.

The horizons of hope also shrank in the USSR, insofar as the 'INNER LIGHT' that can be detected here was all about the dialectical antithesis to the commodity fetish; in general, it concerned human self-consciousness and not a Greek Orthodox, masterless glow—the will-o'-the-wisp of Russia, as it were. The world as a whole, as the movements on the stock markets demonstrated, was wandering all over the place.

Why was the Soviet Union, a sphere cut off from such a world, also affected by it? It looked as if an insanity or desperation, which grips the majority of feelings in the world, also takes hold of a part of mankind organizationally excluded from it, as if there were a sub-industrial current, regulated by the mysterious POLITICAL ECONOMY OF LABOUR, that DETERMINES the sense of the possible (optimism) in human beings. Thus, the same people (or their children and nephews) who drove the fascists from their country in 1944 regarded a takeover of the outlawed and hopeless capital in 1929 as an excessive project that did not deserve their trust. How could the commissars from Baku, imprisoned within the Kremlin walls, win victory without support of the masses?

—Do you believe the collapse of heavy industry, which we observe today in the former Soviet Union and former East Germany, would not have occurred if at that time the world economy had been taken over by working people? Having occupied the commanding heights of capital, would the workers have gone on to produce coal, iron, machine tools, aeroplanes, ships, etc. infinitely?

—Yes, and what's more the continuation of it by other means.

—Would that have been progress or a cul-de-sac?

—An industry with self-confidence is not comparable to the REAL CAPITALIST AGE, which suffered from an inferiority complex.

—That self-confidence departed with the convoy in the hills near Uralsk?

—Yes, because of the international crisis.

—The industrial combines of East Germany would not have been broken up?

—Both moons of Mars would be colonized.

Turkish Honey

It was useless like so much that Bauhaus Dessau, guardian of the PRINCIPLE OF USE in industry, was now dealing with at the turn of the century. Industry, in fact a large part of pre-industrial relations, on which industry was based, had broken away from the institute. Fred Raffert separated himself from his working group. He was interested in a particular question because Christmas was drawing near, a question he had been drawn to by a remark of his father uttered with shining eyes in the hour of his death. It concerned the taste of Turkish honey in 1939. In a small town in central Germany, the pre-war supply of this foodstuff lasted until the Christmas market of 1939.

It was delivered in large forms or tins like a cheese wheel. Its shape emerged out of a mass of honey-sugar-fruit; the portions were scraped from this mass and whisked into fluffy balls. The food was invented in the sixteenth century in Istanbul and reached by way of Viennese confectioners the fairground business at the end of the nineteenth century. In Germany, woodruff flavouring and other hybrid ingredients were added. Whey and substances were added during the First World War; tropical flavourings were also in stock. In the Stefan George Circle, the herbal mixture was called Devil's Flavour. Raffert's father's 'quick' look was part of this historical product. It was no longer possible for him to describe his perception of the taste in precise words. Only the expression on his face spoke to it.

The product belongs to the LOST VARIETIES OF COMMODITY PRODUCTION OF THE CENTURY. What replaced it after 1945 was 'invented'. As soon as there were funfairs again, it bore the name 'Turkish honey', was somehow sweet and mixed with honey. A number of Spanish and French companies attempted to make synthetic versions. Cheaper production did not bring about the same delicious taste that molasses must have created in 1939.

What a terrible shame. Raffert conducted interviews. In a food archive, he found almost half of a 1932 recipe for the production of Turkish honey. Essential parts were missing. What Raffert was able to produce with resources from the Bauhaus did not taste good. The sole authentic clue that remains is his father's 'shining eyes'. Not even in Working Group IV in Dessau, with its experts in industrial reconstruction, could discourse convey or communicate the radiance of that final moment.

The Proprietor

Two Days before His Bankruptcy, Building Contractor Simon Weigel Counts the Seconds of His Life

Northwester over Berlin. Short, fast-flying clouds rhythmize the movement of the moon. Simon Weigel, head of the Gruppe Zentrum Bau S.A. which collapsed the following day (he, however, died two weeks later), had no knowledge of the conclusion to his life as he looked at the dramatic sky from his vehicle. His business associate H. Wedekind insisted on picking him up at the airport in a VW bus with two employees sitting in the third row of seats. Everything intended to underline the importance of the urgent visit.

The weather front covered the plain, which stretched like a uniform landscape as far as the Ural Mountains, and whose large-scale weather patterns also always includes Berlin's sea of buildings. Above the city, however, the weather appears like a parade, as it were, because so many sensitive souls may be suspected in its houses, souls who hear and feel this storm so that the latter is lit up by sentiment much like a search light. The turbulent atmosphere acquires a sense of drama.

Further out, a similarly agitated relationship, observed only by a few, between the moon, clouds and the storm signals god-forsakenness: a swift uninterrupted stream of air, mixed off the Newfoundland coast, has crossed the Atlantic in three or four days as an oceanic accessory and is now treating the continent as if it were a part of the ocean.

That's something money can't buy, says Simon Weigel. They should have projections running in the foyers of the office blocks they're building on Friedrichstraße that reproduce this nocturnal mood 'northwester over Berlin'. Even on the hottest August day, such projections would create a longing for a solid roof over one's head. The craving for luxurious accommodations and a secure, warm office space in Berlin Mitte was not what it might be at the moment.

Weather conditions like these have occurred over Berlin since the turn of the eighteenth to the nineteenth centuries, each lasting up to three days. They occurred a total of 19,992 times, i.e. twelve times a year. Observed by men of action whose sensitivities were impoverished, they become rare. Either such a man sees nothing, or he is not sensitive that day, or he is not in Berlin, or he is not an entrepreneurial man of action. If he is not a man of action, then his heart is moved but his actions are not influenced because he for example only writes poetry or runs around or observes a break in his life.

Hitler saw such a moon in the stormy month of November in 1936. Napoleon observed it during his brief stay in Berlin in 1806. Bismarck mentions it six times in his *Reflections and Reminiscences*; no doubt he saw it more often than that. Strousberg, the railway king, saw it seven months before the bankruptcy of his imperium. The Siemens Brothers did not take note of it, even though they saw it: they were preparing to set up companies in Baku and in the vicinity of Tangier; it's not the case, however, that a 'cloudy moon' is a prediction of good or bad luck. Lives are too short to be strongly impacted by the lasting influence of the moon, which only has long-term effects. Only over a span of fourteen generations, given perfect memory and constant energy on the part of the individual members of these generations, would the moon be fate. This would correspond to roughly half the individual life of a giant. Today, however, we seldom talk about giants, at best we talk about giant cities.[41]

---

41 Dante Alighieri calculates the height of a giant to be 122.5 metres. He assumes that the distance from his, Dante's, hand to his elbow is 50 cm. Seventy times that would be 35 metres. The ratio of the distance between hand and elbow to total body height is 1:3.5. Dante, who conducted this investigation, was something between stocky and small in stature. The figures are given in Galileo's *The Measurement of Hell*

The company that Simon Weigel owned was 110 years old. The business it carried on had changed twice. In two inflations in the same century, it had been cut back to its tangible assets and thus revitalized. In 1989, the cautious Weigel had been faced by temptation. Day and night, he drove in a rented car up and down the country roads of the still-sovereign GDR. He had instigated joint ventures, conspiracies with company workforces, of which the organs of the dying state were no longer aware. The concept he was pursuing: A third of the property for the workforce, a third for further development or the local authority, a third for the investor or entrepreneur. A diversity of property, so to speak, a variety of characters of property, classified according to use values. In a race with the unsupervised legislator (this changed from the People's Chamber to local councils and then to Bonn) and his competition advancing on a broad front, who had already held initial talks with the Provisional Administrator of State Property before Weigel noticed the new jurisdictions, Weigel won and lost, obstinacy sacrificed part of his own fortune, wanted the spoils lying around free (only at first sight), just like in 1945 when as a boy he had picked up aeroplane parts in the Junkers caves, saw himself impeded, struggled and, on the day of the currency reform in the former East Germany, was reduced to a few, albeit choice locations in the metropolis of the country. Here, a rapid connection to the market currents of Western Europe seemed possible. Since then, Simon Weigel's group of companies had been concentrating on these remaining objects

---

According to Dante Alighieri from 1587. Since the spatial and time measurements of all living things develop proportionately, the lifetime of a giant in ancient times comes to 420 years. A deduction must be made to take account of the fact that the astral body of a human being only continues growing until the third year; after that, human bodies develop no more than an empty shell; they represent a phenomenon that should not be assumed to be the independent giants of ancient times.

including a number of construction projects in central Berlin. Demand was growing too slowly. In the course of this forced march, he had lost—along with a large part of his wealth—his faith in the freedom of trade, in planning, in parts of his charm; he found himself acting more like a rescue worker and less like an entrepreneur.

Under the flickering moonlight (= moon interrupted by bits of cloud), they reached the district lying east of Alexanderplatz and behind Frankfurter Straße. They inspected excavated sites. One had to imagine tall buildings there. It was further possible to imagine the development of Alexanderplatz, a coming and going of building inspectors, the completed seat of government in the bend of the River Spree, a tunnel under the city centre, the preservation of transportation, international interests, a *fräulein* miracle in the East resulting in the revival of the erotic horizon of the still-grey city that was previously criss-crossed by construction sites, and thus greed, thriftiness and an abstract hedonism arise, producing gravitational forces that are the precondition for the enterprise called success. Nothing of this propulsive power or even gravitation that was suggested in the illustrated brochures of the project really existed yet. A sort of poetic activity was required in order to imagine 'the step-by-step development of motifs in the course of construction', the emergence of the necessary mental confusion and creative destruction. The prerequisite for this was to drive foreign companies and people into this city centre, to get them to leave their ancestral homes and to try their luck here in this imaginary space. 'The next generation will build on the ruins of our projects.'[42] Simon Weigel felt afraid.

---

42 Albert Speer on the destruction of buildings in the bend of the Spree, which in 1941 created room for the planning of the new Reich capital Berlin. This Reich capital, renamed Germania, had its centre in public buildings in the bend of the Spree. The basic idea of the plan was a gigantic north–south axis.

He had been swept along by the spirit emanating from the beginnings in December 1989, when the quarry lay there for the taking, not for anyone but for the quick and the creative. That was the haul, a relatively small but perfectly preserved behemoth[43] that, while it was still disintegrating into its living parts, was suddenly slain and split up in a flash. Removed from those gnawing on it, it sat in the hands of senior civil servants, coalitions of auditors and big companies.

In the tremendous howling of the gale, the building sites now looked empty, empty of immediate hope. Even in the face of imminent defeat, Simon Weigel still held onto the role of 'leading shaker and maker' as if he were a resolute actor. He asked questions and made gestures. It was no longer important what exactly he demonstrated. In a few days, his leadership was over; the bank representatives divided up his 'fish', set them up for new creative destruction in Schumpeter's sense. Beginners would start new attempts to bridge time until the foundations for free-enterprise success had been established in this part of the world. Simon Weigel knew that by then he would no longer be counted among the living in the capitalist sense. What he didn't know is that inside himself forces of decline were organizing themselves so that his fortune would rapidly be followed by his human body.

A full human life contains about 36,000 days. Simon Weigel looked back on 18,200 days. Even if one deducts from that a childhood devoid of memories and the days of most intense agitation, which destroy memory and with it 'retrospection', he would have been unable to account for how he had spent or individually invested them. He could only vaguely orientate himself

43 It is known that the proto-animals Leviathan and Behemoth (like a shoal of fish or a swarm of locusts) form a whole out of living parts. These unities never fell apart so swiftly that the parts gained a life of their own before they were swept up in the demise of another one of the animals.

in his own past. Topography of time disposed of: On the plane, in anticipation of his birthday that was in two months' time, he had entered into his laptop a rough breakdown of the years. To that end, it is possible to use the succession of places where one has stayed at Christmas or New Year. On such holidays, Simon Weigel never stayed at home, i.e. the trips differentiated the years. Another indicator: the development of the company and its data, conspicuous results. A third indicator: a few moments of happiness; when was I boundlessly happy for seconds or minutes? The deaths of great politicians or political turning points, on the other hand, gave only very imprecise assistance with the breakdown of one's own time. Simon just about knew *where* he was when he heard the news of Kennedy's death.

At last, he reached his hotel. An Italian designer had the interior of the large building completely done in blue. The carpets in the rooms and corridors display the dominant colour in various shades. The basic idea is simple: It's the visual translation of the name 'Maritim'. This large building, too, is waiting on the future development of the city.

How does a loser feel when he arrives in his suite, the double bed in sight, in the dim light, sheltered from the storm and fast-changing moonlight by thick blue curtains reminiscent of big city drapes in bourgeois villas from the turn of the century? Simon Weigel shuts the door, unpacks, takes a hot shower. A bad headache torments him whenever there's an extreme temperature change.

He reads in bed for a couple of minutes and falls asleep. He will do all this while still awake, more or less consciously, and then he breathes out the last of his elan. His scattered habits, which he carries with him every day like clothes in a suitcase, will remain behind, unclaimed when he sets out again.

There are six clocks in the room including his watch. He's been wearing it on his wrist now for thirty years. Like keen guard dogs, they measure the seconds and minutes. Regarding those minutes, Simon Weigel will have 18,200 times 24 times 60 = 26,208,000 to show for in the balance sheet of his life. That makes for 18,200 times 24 times 60 times 60 blinks in his life, assuming one reckons a second for each one of Simon Weigel's, to his friends, unmistakeable flickers of an eye. That is realistic, even if a scare or a final blink closes his eye in less than a second. But it is a miscalculation to the extent that during sleep, as now, his eyelids may twitch while essentially remaining shut at night. To Simon Weigel, sleep is no 'little death', but rather a down payment on the independent existence of his kidneys, liver, beating heart, circulation and dreams, but also the self-regulating forces in his head, which he felt as intense shooting pains before he fell asleep and which, pulsing along with his blood, are dangerous, intangible opponents, less tangible than his bank opponents and competitors who want to destroy him the day after tomorrow. He has resolved to keep his composure; it's the only property he has left.

A Dignified Form of Property: Time

THE TOOTH OF TIME

As both a user of the Internet and someone committed to modernity, I refuse, dentist Dr Erwin Peikert from Oschersleben near Halberstadt said, to spend more than a minute and a half on the news. I've diverted time from my career and my life. What's more, I fear that I'll miss out on other news also of potential interest while I'm still watching this news. Since such short-winded consumption doesn't captivate me, I often stop watching before the minute-and-thirty-second mark is over. I am a 'passionate user'.

TEMPO ORDINARIO (A NATURAL TIME INTERVAL)

The 'natural' beat, from which faster and slower tempi can be distinguished, is the heartbeat. Johann Sebastian Bach always placed the finger of his right hand on his left wrist before beginning a concert. City councillors who saw this thought it was a quirk. Yet the master checked the tempo for the music, which he imagined in his head, using his thumb and forefinger against the corporeal music, which he alone trusted. For this purpose, a watch would have been of no use to him.

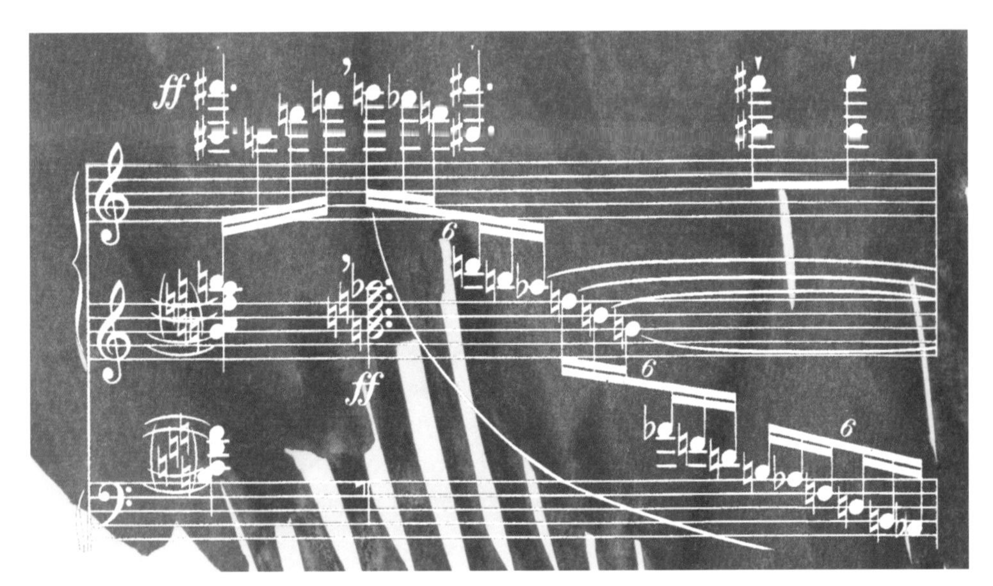

FIGURE 29. Modernist notation from an opera by Alban Berg. With a watercolour by Katharina Grosse. Printed on aluminium, 2020.

FIGURE 30. 'An allegory of music fires an arrow at a dragon'.

THE TIME OF LANGUAGES

'The last speaker of about half of all languages spoken in the world is alive today.' Linguist K. D. Harrison formulated this sentence in reference to languages, the lifespans of which have lasted longer than a thousand years. A Berlin programmer used the wonderfully flexible language FLASH to make an artwork recently acquired for the collection at Princeton University's library. The programming language didn't survive more than a decade. 'It's no longer supported.' Its successor, HTML5, looks forward to a similarly brief lifespan.

THE MISERLINESS OF TIME

A farmer from the agrarian age waits during winter. He has plenty of time. He even takes breaks during the harvest, as long as storms are far away. Generations change slowly.

A chronicler of the bourgeois epoch—it's only been around for a short time and already seems to be over—records an ENORMOUS COMPRESSION OF TIME. Nothing of this property, which only death puts limits on, shall go unused. Joseph Conrad was as such restless on his journey to the Congo, eager to gain time so he can travel back home again and share what he experienced.

Thomas Mann intended to write a book on the ACCOUNTING OF TIME. He abandoned the project on account of the diversity of the material. What remained was his report about an Englishman who travelled by steamboat up the Yellow River during a muggy, unpleasant summer and appraised with his British eyes various objects of value on either bank of the river. This sort of sightseeing sufficed for the purposes of his joint-stock company back home. It's possible to borrow stockpiled intentions for future actions on the London Stock Exchange.

In early August 2011, one of the EXPERIENCED TAMERS OF CAPITAL sat in a tower in one of Frankfurt's skyscrapers. He had eyes only for his computer screen. At this elevation over the city, the blinding glare of the sun was muted by an adjustable screen over the windows. On the computer screens, very little was recognizable. It looked as if the room itself was wearing a pair of sunglasses.

On this day, the experts didn't know how to be of assistance. They saw the market crash graphically in the form of a vertical line signalizing the DAX's loss of 4 percentage points in 4 minutes. That corresponded to a value of a few billion dollars. The practitioner possessed no theory for the events as they transpired in the dimly lit room above the city. Does the lion tamer have a theory? He knows his animals. This creature's behaviour, responsible for causing monstrous destruction on both sides of the Atlantic, was unknown to the experts. Was this a new species? Or was it the crisis of 1929 dressed up differently? The legendary man in his boardroom, the man who otherwise knows how to bridle markets, would gladly have reacted to the events in a practical fashion: crack a few nuts, peel an apple, pour a glass of sparking water. He wanted contact to any old activity if it meant he didn't have to stare at the screen and wait.

FIGURE 31. The constellation of the hippopotamus.

FIGURE 32. The pharaoh's scribe.

LIVED TIME FOR CASH

A worker in Frankfurt am Main spent his whole life in one and the same factory. The factory went bankrupt. The employees were let go. The worker visited a doctor. He had a severe stomach ache long before the factory shut its doors. The doctor prescribed him medication. I devoted countless days of my life, the worker said, and as a reward I get these pills. I'm not OK with this. You shouldn't hang your head, the doctor consoled him. I don't even have the energy to fuel my anger, the worker replied. This isn't a fair exchange: lived time for cash.

A HISTORICAL SECOND

The Reich Chancellor, Adolf Hitler, speaks to me. I am one of his assistants. I'm supposed to deliver a note within five minutes on how the German Reich can advance to the Pacific by way of Greece, Cyprus and Aden. The chancellor had before him a study by the German Naval Warfare Command. The files can now be found in the National Archives in Washington under the designation 'Grand Design'. Military planning in the spring of 1942 envisaged a push by German troops from Africa and the Balkans toward Suez and Aden, which would later lead to a meeting with the Japanese war fleet and cooperation between these allies in the Pacific. Unfortunately, I had consumed a few rounds of schnapps in the Führer's bunker canteen and, at this decisive moment in my life, wasn't my usual sociable self, according to my friend E. I spent three minutes contemplating, one minute developing a concept and, five minutes later still, was not finished writing the text. The Führer said, Well, have you come up anything yet? I had to reply, You'll have it in a few minutes, my Führer. He said, I don't have that much time.

Calls came in. I stumbled across one of those MOMENTS OF DESTINY that Hitler biographer Kershaw writes about. I am still convinced that in these moments of hesitation I could have introduced a concept that would have given the Second World War and the fortunes of the Reich a different turn.

I still regret today (and will have a note of this put on my tombstone) that I failed in that 'historical second', which, as I said already, lasted roughly five minutes (after seven and a half minutes I wasn't able to follow up because of the phone calls).

A HALBERSTADTIAN MEASUREMENT OF TIME

In April 1945, Hartmut Eisert from Halberstadt was thirteen years old. Back then he got a haircut irregularly, that is when the hairdresser in town was open and his parents told him to. Later, when he was in his twenties, he got a haircut once every eight weeks, which gave the passing of years and life itself an imperceptible if not faint beat. This rhythm changed by a few days and even sometimes a week before holidays and vacations. In such moments, the frequency of haircuts increased. Sometimes a haircut brings with it luck. Sometimes it is the beginning of a period of indifference in a person's life. Hartmut was superstitious. It was bad when a haircut was bungled (by a new, inexperienced hairdresser).

Until his death in 2014, he will experience approximately 560 haircuts. When he goes to get his haircut, he only wears 'reliable' clothes, in other words, clothes that once already brought him good luck. A bad haircut can spoil 1/560th of his life, provided he knows when his end will come. The shock he gets when seeing his butchered hair in the mirror is tempered by the fact that he knows nothing of the hour of his death.

A BIT RADIOACTIVE

I received a 'grown-up' watch for my eighth birthday. It was quite chunky and heavy and hung on my young arm: numbers made from phosphor fluoresced a bright green in the dark. Today, I don't know whether a radioactive substance on a child's arm was safe. Faithful as a dog, the watch accompanied me when I played in school, in my sleep and during air raids. It brought me luck because I didn't perish in the war. On 8 April 1945, of all days, I didn't put the watch on. I took it off that morning to wash. It was the Sunday after Easter. I got dressed quickly. After breakfast, I would change clothes and prepare myself for the day. The air-raid siren interrupted all my plans. The city was reduced to rubble in twenty-five minutes.

The luminous watch, along with my favourite sweater, remained behind in my childhood room. Those things, which constituted part of my gear, were on the third floor of my parents' home that was to burn to the ground within a few hours. In fact, I later searched the mass of bricks—the property now in ruins—to look for the watch, a sturdy imperial German replica of a Swiss model. I had faith that it survived even under these circumstances. Even today I am sure the watch ticked for a long time deep underneath the rubble (it had been freshly wound the evening prior). Nevertheless, in the darkness deep beneath the stones, perhaps from within a cavity, the luminous numbers (a bit radioactive and lethal) cast their light for a long time and convey the time of day to whomever it may concern.

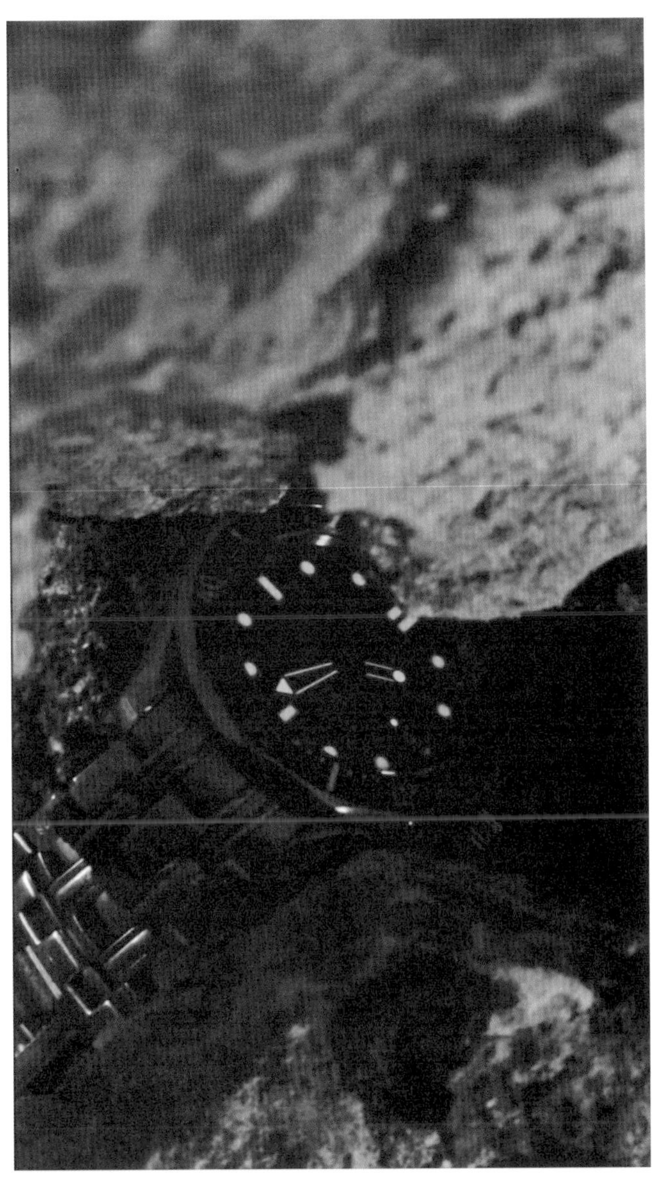

FIGURE 33. My watch with luminous numerals beneath the rubble of our house.

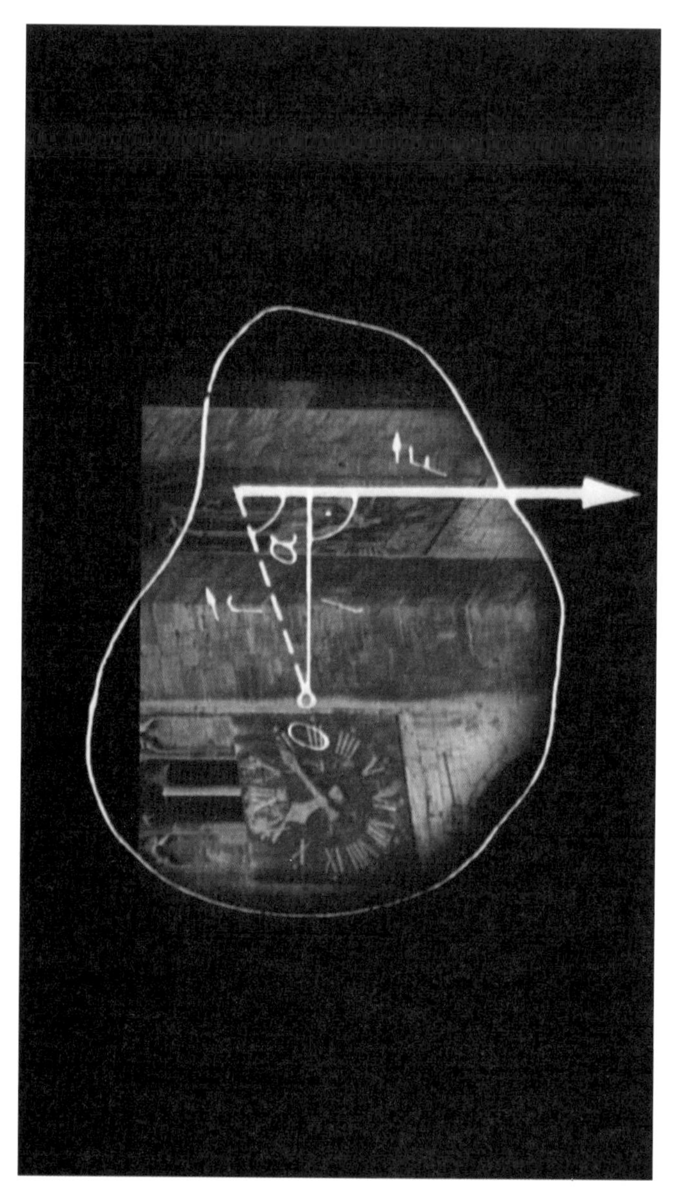

FIGURE 34. The clock at St Martini in Halberstadt. Together with an illustration by Paul Klee: My grandfather checked his pocket watch against this clock every day. The hands of the church clock stopped at 11.10 a.m. This is when the first bomb exploded near the church on 8 April 1945.

OWNERSHIP OF ONE'S LIFE SPAN

My maternal grandmother Martha Blackburn had taken an afternoon nap. At this late moment in her life, she could maintain her habit of lying down, but she could no longer fall asleep. She brooded over death. On the one hand, she discussed from her bed with the sleepy visitor shifting his weight on the couch across from her just how willing she was to accept the fact that there could be life after death. On the other hand, she doesn't want to make herself look ridiculous when she says that to others or even merely accepts it internally. She doesn't want to make a fool of herself either. Conversely, she wishes not to head for death without any hope at all. She's tough, I replied consolingly, her grandson. I wanted to keep sleeping.

'IT WILL BE SPRING LIKE THIS AGAIN IN A HUNDRED YEARS'

They didn't sit on a bench. It wasn't spring either. Here, at Café Westkamp, a kind of permanent twilight was created using soft indirect lighting that made a person's skin tone and eyes shine. A person felt younger and more attractive in this gentle light rich with illusions. At the same time, one felt inwardly illuminated by an uninterrupted sequence of hit songs that reached one's ears in the afternoon from record players and loudspeakers and in the evenings from lively artists performing on stage.

The couple met one another for the first time yesterday afternoon and have remained together ever since. They hummed along to the song that had just been recorded:

> 'It will be spring like this
> again in a hundred years'

This was followed by 'and we will never be'. The lyrics assumed that a hundred years from now spring would look similar to what it is today and that the couple would sit side by side on a bench by a body of water and (imaginatively) be able to catch a glimpse of another pair of lovers sitting in their place ('same bench, but unfortunately other people'). That didn't make them sad in Café Westkamp, but rather thoughtful, since they still had plenty of time before it got too late in the evening, at which point they would have to hurry to their respective trains and take leave of one another.

—Are spring seasons likely to be the same in a hundred years as they are today?

—It's autumn. How should I know? I believe every spring is unique. Every day is different.

—Would you recognize me if we met again 'as different people'? Do you think we reappear in this world?

—The difficulty will be to find each other. How do I recognize you?

—Would you like to?

—Very much so.

—Just like you think today?

—Just like today as in a hundred years.

—Does it have to be spring?

—At any time of the year, for example, in autumn.

—Will Germany rule the world?

—That's independent of that.

These 'days from long ago' triggered strong feelings in the couple. Simultaneously, they debated how to arrange another meeting in the shortest possible time on the tracks of their draft orders (she was to report to a munitions plant and he to the Eastern Front).

The Reich's network of controls was so airtight that they couldn't hope to stray from their duties of their own free will (deserting out of love for one another). Were a dragnet put out for them such that they had to seek shelter in some hiding place, that was worse than prison. How soothing the song that made them believe they were transported to a certain season a hundred years from now. By 6 p.m. they had not yet made plans for quickly seeing each other again. There wasn't enough time for any intimacy again before saying goodbye. They approached the record player and put the music back on. The staff accepted the lonely couple's arbitrariness and let them do as they liked.

THE MAN IN A HURRY

He didn't forgive anyone for mistakes. Nature didn't forgive him either. He's now only forty-seven years old. For years he lay in wait for the top position at Merrill Lynch, but no one promoted the American to it. His leadership style hampered his rise. A large European bank poached him. Fifty employees followed him from Merrill Lynch to his new employer, and that spoke volumes for him. After a year, his management contributed two-thirds of the bank's profits that the bank had entrusted to him.

He was considered eccentric. That belongs, said his confidant Maximilian von Kemper, to his preferred TYPE OF REPRESENTATION; in principle, he had no time for a personal characteristic like eccentricity.

With the Concorde he flew from London to his dentist in New York. Why not? Surgery on one's physical integrity is of utmost importance and worth the few hours for the Atlantic crossing. His weekly visits to his family also entailed transatlantic flights. When he flew, nothing could happen to the plane. He was lucky.

The mouth a line. Penetrating clear eyes just five minutes after waking up from a night's sleep. Pointed ears pulled up, as seen on riders, lying close to the head but set at an angle, streamlined. Pretty dimples on the cheeks where stars see them, but slides down towards the base of the chin. By the time he's fifty, said a plastic surgeon who saw him, that face will look fat; this is due to the tension emanating from your mouth giving the orders. Under the nose a spacious gutter where nothing flows.

A mother raised him like that. Colby College and Dartmouth University trained him like that. The bottleneck of time began with the departure of Merrill Lynch.

Five years in the yoke of time. A single individual living being has only five years to maintain economic power like that of Louis Shrivers. The years before were necessary to get the position; the years after were needed to defend it and to organize his exit. Shrivers didn't manage to last the full five years.

The bank's Christmas parties in London with hostesses were notorious. It was absurd to think that he himself had had time to attract companions. To that extent, he was selfless. He was well protected, as long as he worked in the field of art like his many colleagues, the 'established and practised business.' 'THAT'S NOT POSSIBLE IF IT DOESN'T EXIST' was his motto. He succeeded in integrating Bankers Trust, a US banking empire, into a European bank, violently and effectively.[44] Not just acquisition, but rather the power and depth of penetration, that was his reputation.

Like when one's breath stops out of fear, time was running out for him before Christmas Eve. Had he been Catholic or had his family been used to a Roman Christmas celebration, then there would have been plenty of time before the first Christmas holiday, which fell on a Monday that year, to reach his family

---

44 In contrast to BMW's 'weak' takeover of Rover.

gathered at a weekend home in Maine, USA. For Protestants, however, Christmas Eve is traditionally a festive event. Louis Shrivers raced in by skipping over the Atlantic. For the final leg from Portland to his home in the mountains, he took off in a twin-engine Beach 2000. Steven Bean, his personal pilot, had flown in from New York. The plane's path got lost along the Maine coast. The wreck was found in the immediate vicinity of the Beaver Mountains. Three meters in front of the plane, the body of the man in a hurry[45] penetrated the swampy ground of the peat bog. The on-duty sheriff confirmed that the pilot was also killed immediately.

NORTH OF EDEN

In a town north of Lake Michigan where blizzards fill the place with snow more than twice a year, life goes slow. Police officer Patterson struggled through the rest of his life.

Years ago, he had met a Finnish woman in this solitary place. The daughter born of this union perished. She was three years old. Patterson's wife had run hot water in the bathtub without mixing any cold water in yet. She was called to the phone. She ran downstairs, hurriedly made a call. The curious child, just leaning against the tub, fell into the water. Driven to the clinic forty kilometres away with scalded skin, the little creature fought for its life for several days and nights. While Patterson was taking care of the burial, his wife shot herself with a hunting rifle.

For a long time, the police officer seemed 'disconnected from reality'. He remains inextricably linked to the dead girl, said his superior McFerguson. As if he were waiting to follow the two he lost.

---

45 He was one of the very few bankers to be paid largely in cash rather than in stock options.

Did he attempt to bring them back? No, he didn't find the entrance to the underworld. This entrance is not in the part of the world where Patterson lived. The place where such an entrance exists, namely, in the vicinity of Naples, was entirely unfamiliar to him. Also, his manager said, he would have missed the blizzards and would have felt uncertain in Italian hotels. Did he go there? Once. He returned without having accomplished anything. He had read all the manuals on how to behave at the gates of Hades. He lined up the volumes in his hut. When he arrived at the entrance, he would hardly have made a mistake.

What prevented him from killing himself? The same ties that bound him to the dead woman. He had seen something of life, a sign worth living. In principle, he couldn't let that go.

Was he hoping for a new bond? How was that supposed to come about up here in the short days of summer? Who came here as a stranger? He was not open to compromises.

His superior reported that many were trying to get at him. Was he useful as a police officer? Hardly. He was absent. He didn't even seem reliable as a driver. On the other hand, there was no salient reason for his dismissal, especially since the official deficits had existed for a long time. He was fed at the expense of the community. Someone has to pay for the grieving.

DAY TIME, EARTHLY TIME AND THE 'TIME BENEATH OUR SKIN'

I see the hands of my watch. What we measure with clocks is a COUNTER-IMAGE of time; time itself doesn't look like a clock. Time doesn't have a specific 'look' at all. Time creeps, it quarrels and interrupts itself in its course, it condenses into knots, makes history, withdraws into itself, bobs up and down, disappears into the earth like water in a swamp. Waiting period. 'I'm still running, the train is running away from me. Later, I hear that it crashed. There were severely injured and dead. I couldn't grab time by its hair. It saved me . . . ?'

Atomic clocks measure time accurately. Clocks operating on the level of quanta and quarks: Like parallel computers or separate worlds, times and their measuring devices, the clocks, move side by side. CROSS MAPPING. The two kinds of precision—the one we ascribe to the nature of time and the other we use to measure this nature—have edged over the course of history towards extreme convergence. Even though they are still worlds apart and I'm not sure the time is 'exact'.

Time is sluggish, it's multi-directional. It's the master of extreme acceleration. It's dynamic. It has its own beat. It is opposed to everything that is NOT TIME. Aside from looking at watches, I see time on my skin, on my face and on my arms: they are age wrinkles. Do I hear how time flies? In Richard Wagner's *Tristan*, they sing: 'Do I hear the light?' Are such expressions fantastic?

'Reasonable Time'. This is the time of life. Between birth and death: that is equivalent to going to the hairdresser about 750 times in one's life. Another counter for economists is an annual balance sheet. There were five-year plans in the socialist era and there were four-year plans in the Third Reich. Helmut Kohl's chancellorship encompassed several four-year periods.

COSMIC TIME

'You and me and all the stars we can see / Are moving one million miles a day!'

Such cosmic time is vastly different from what constitutes a minute, an hour or a human life. And yet the trillions of cells in our body are closely related and 'entwined' with the stuff of rotating suns and galaxies. There, in cosmic time, elements emerge from elementary particles that suns eject into space when they explode, elements that are indispensable to the building of cells in our body.

Painters traditionally paint in perspective. They also paint anti-perspectively to rebel against the central perspective characteristic of the classics. TIME PERSPECTIVES enter the narration of our present. There is no central perspective of time. There is also no UNIFIED TIME. We live in a ZOO OF TIMES. Subjective and objective. A CHRONO-PLURIVERSE. 'Time breeds monsters.' It does that when we misjudge it, when we don't treat it according to its nature.

FIGURE 35. 'Cosmic Time'. In the background: numerous galaxies in the asterism COMA BERENICES.

GALAXY SONG
galaxy_song00000
galaxy_song00001
"The sun and you and me
and all the stars
that we can see /
galaxy_song00002
Are moving at a million
miles a day..."
Monty Python,
Galaxy Song
galaxy_song00003
galaxy_song00004
galaxy_song00005
galaxy_song00006
galaxy_song00007

FIGURE 36

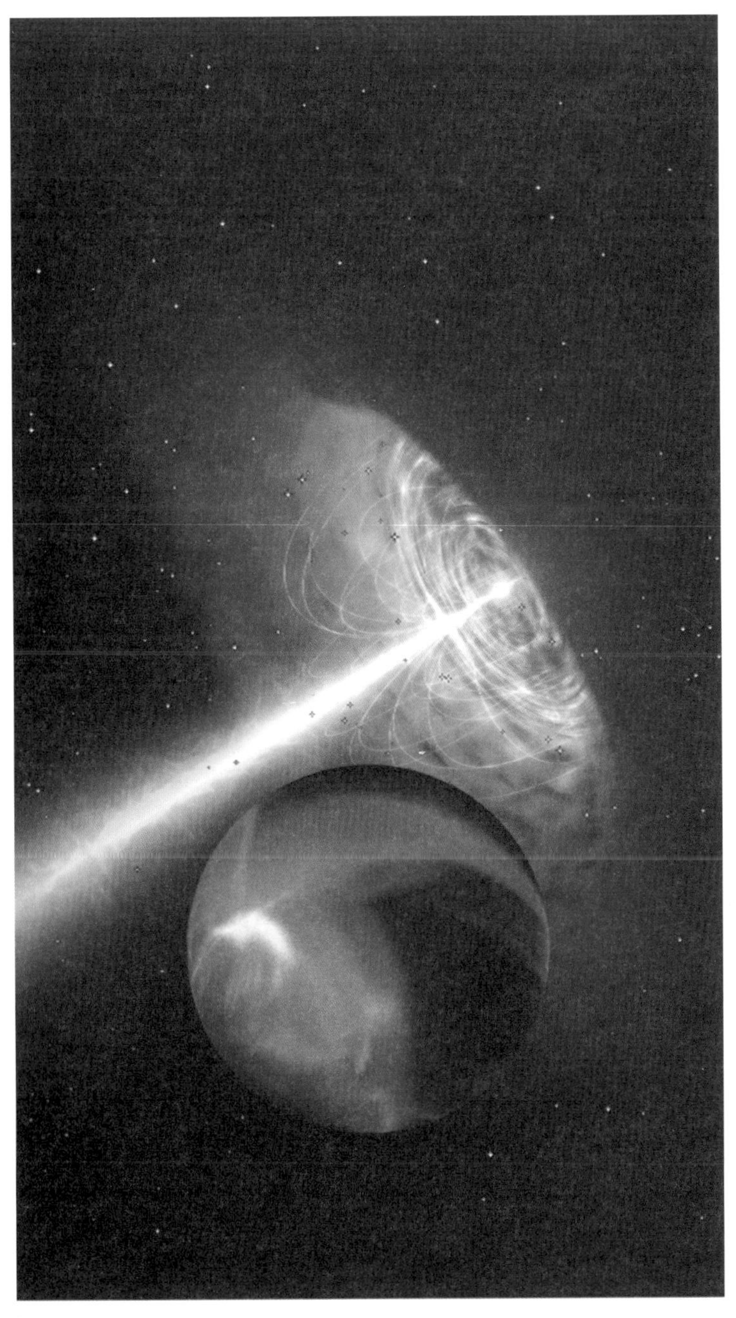

FIGURE 37. A celestial body sprays elementary particles in the form of a JET into open space.

FIGURES 38, 39. Film still from: Katharina Grosse and Alexander Kluge Atopic Cinema, 2020.

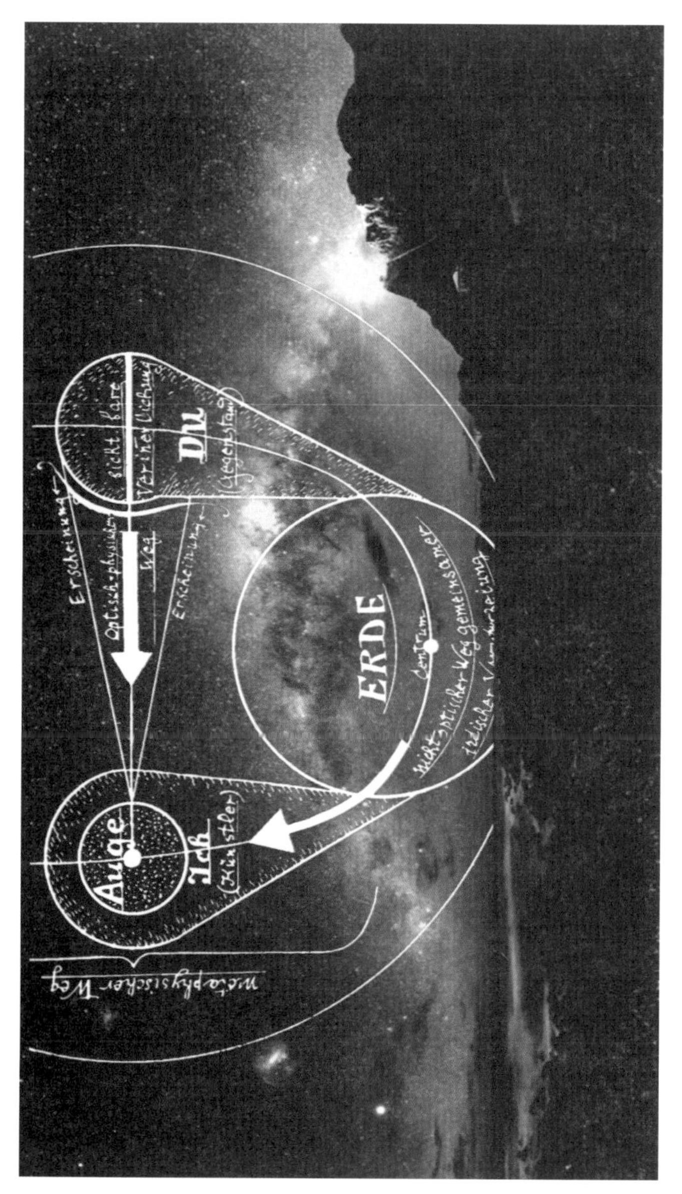

FIGURE 40. Film still, 2020

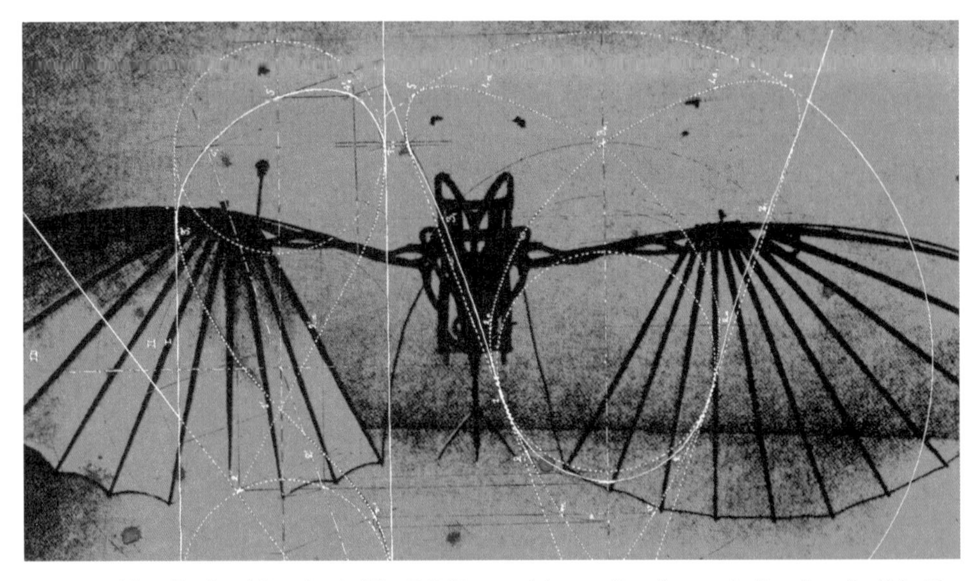

FIGURE 41. A bat. The heraldic animal of the Enlightenment. In a matter of seconds, it emits calls. Using the echoes it receives with its outsized ears it navigates in the dark. Film still printed on aluminium, 2020.

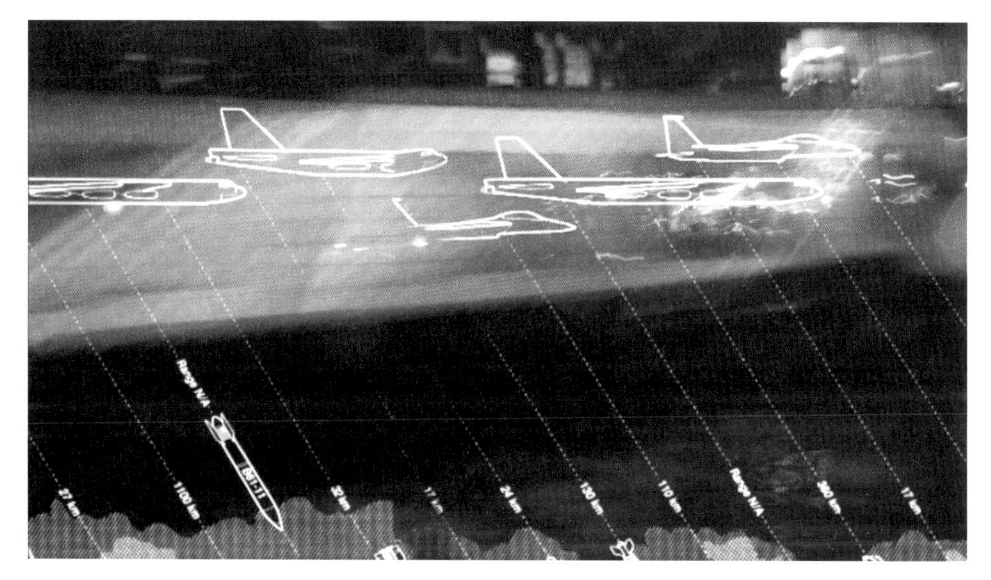

FIGURE 42. 'A measure of time in a bombing war'. Long wait times in an air-raid shelter. Bomb explosions every second.

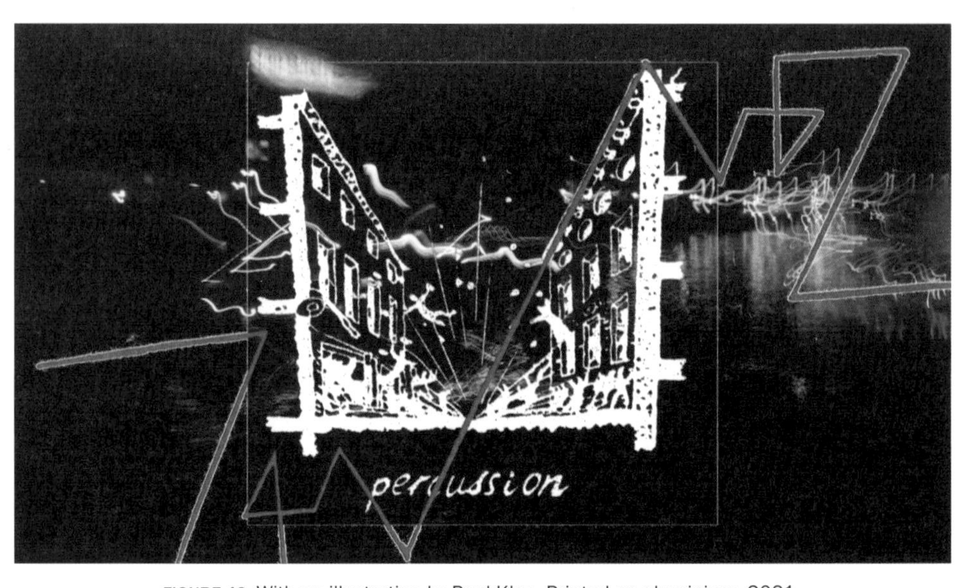

FIGURE 43. With an illustration by Paul Klee. Printed on aluminium, 2021.

FIGURE 44. People in an air-raid shelter in Berg-Karabach. The depths smart bombs can penetrate. Printed on aluminium. Film still, 2021.

FIGURE 45. A mural by cave dwellers. Approximately 40,000 years before Christ. Our ancestors developed dance, empathy and the 'human capacity for imagination' back then. They reached agreements using calls, mimicry, movement and rhythm. They invented language. Grammar came only later. The figures in the cave painting appear to float.

FIGURE 46. 'An allegory of music'.

FIGURE 47. 'The soul bathes in music'.

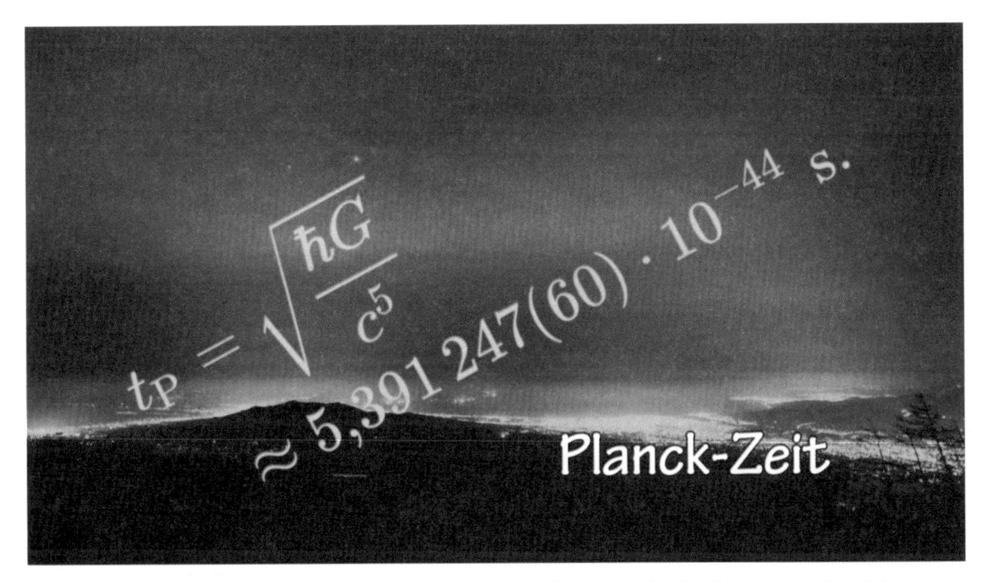

FIGURES 48, 49. A string theory formula on an 'elephant skin' by Anselm Kiefer. A homage to his string theory exhibition in London's White Cube. Film still, 2020.

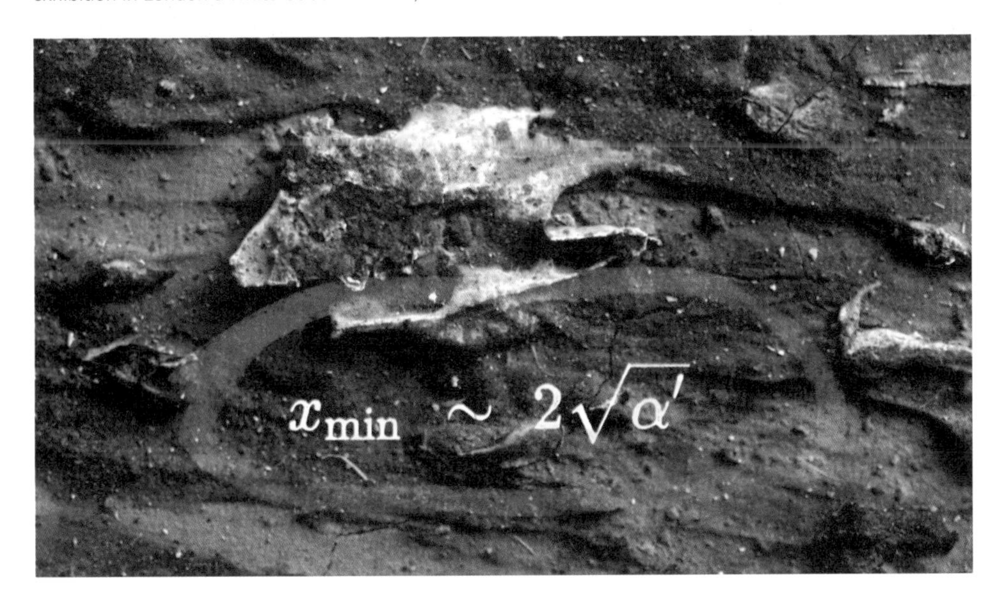

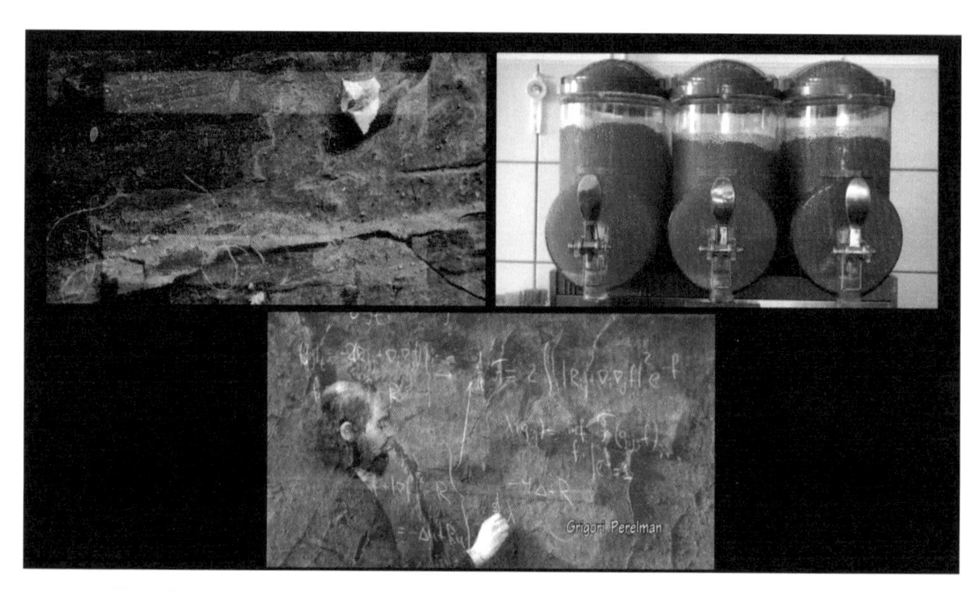

FIGURE 50. From *Gestein der Zeichen*. A triptych film for Anselm Kiefer made on the occasion of his exhibition at White Cube. Below: the Russian mathematician Grigori Perelman. Top right: drink dispensers in Perelman's St Petersburg home.

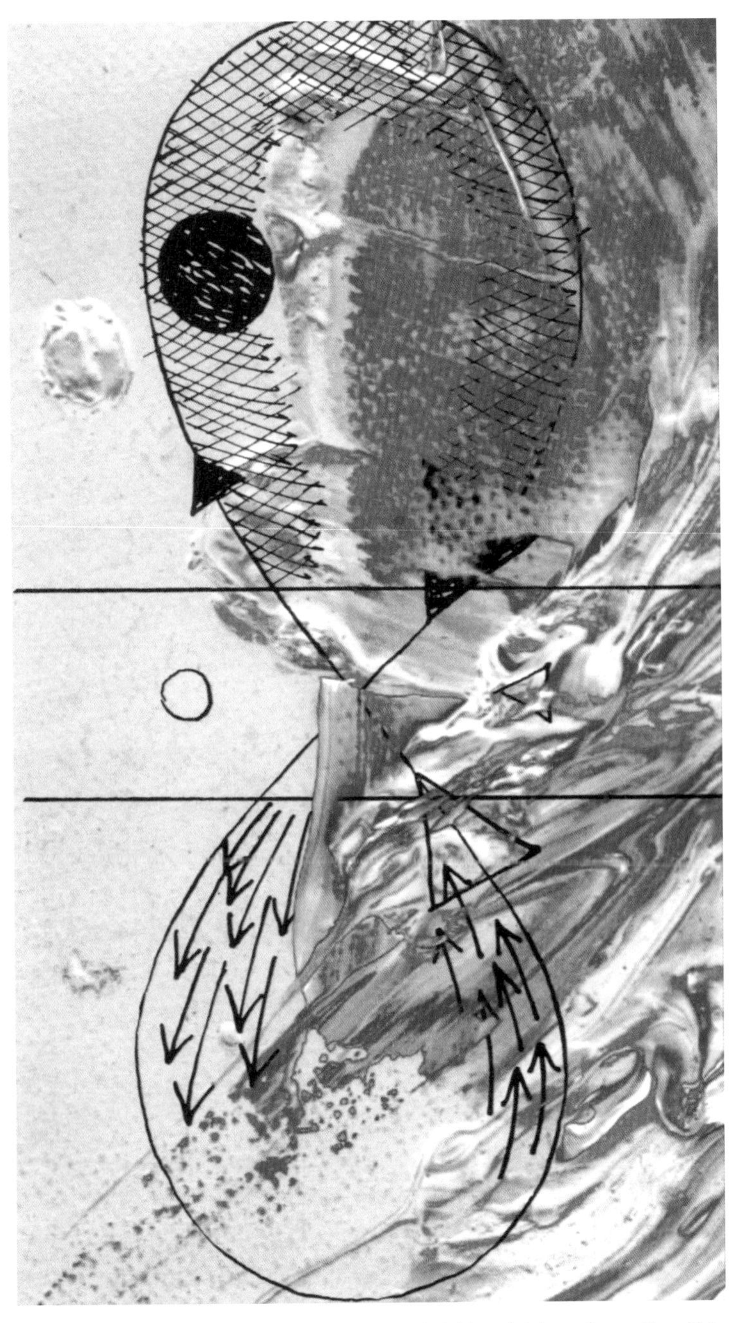

FIGURE 51. 'Time travelling along its many paths'. Material from Georg Baselitz's studio. Film still, 2020.

FIGURE 52. Time perspective from the pyramids backwards to the year 2020: '4,000 years look back at us.' Material from Georg Baselitz's studio together with an illustration by Paul Klee. Film still, 2022.

FIGURE 53. 'The moment of detonation'. A cannon in Stalingrad. An image by Wigand Wüster together with an illustration by Paul Klee. 'Ursache' = cause; 'Wirkung' = action. Film still, 2020.

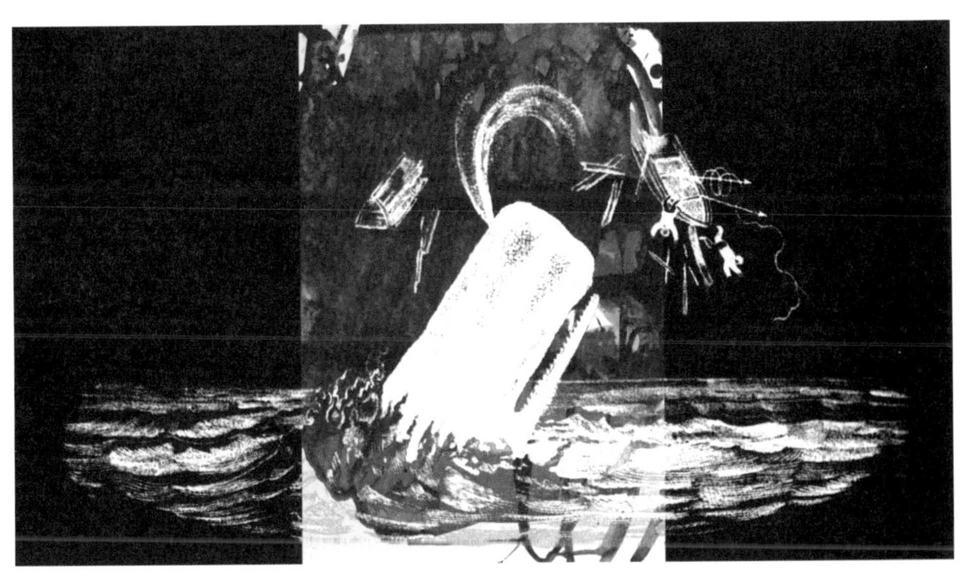

FIGURE 54. Moby Dick hurls the whaler's skiff into the air. 'A matter of seconds'.

FIGURE 55. 'In a matter of seconds the circus dancer balances herself atop a horse standing firmly on a tight-rope'. A background from Georg Baselitz's studio with a motif by Goya. Film still, 2020.

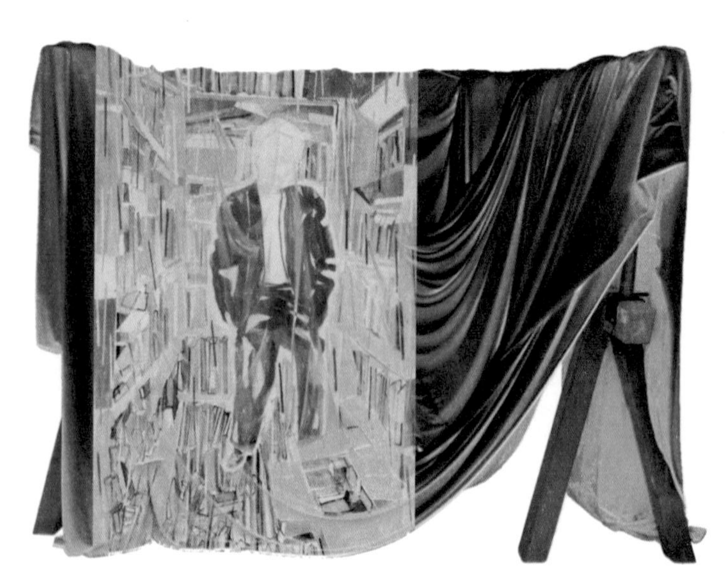

FIGURE 56. A portrait of the author. An image by Thomas Hartmann projected onto Stage No. 3 by Katharina Grosse, 2020